I0760443

THREE SCORCHED KINGDOMS

ACCIDENTAL ALCHEMY
BOOK THREE

HEATHER HILDENBRAND

Three Scorched Kingdoms

Accidental Alchemy #3

Cover Design by Covers by Christian

Proofread by Dawn Y

www.heatherhildenbrand.com

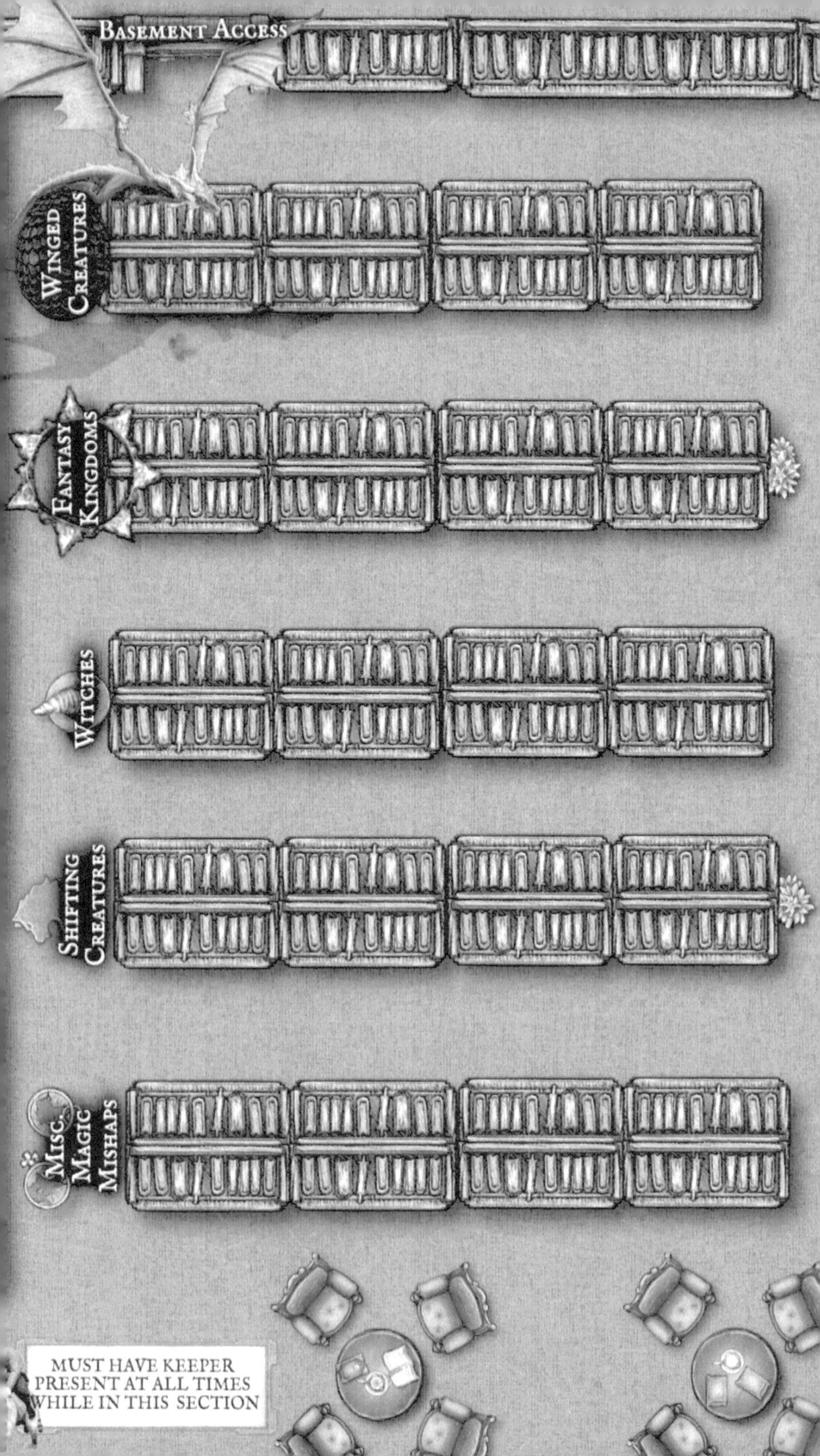

Basement Access
Winged Creatures
Fantasy Kingdoms
Witches
Shifting Creatures
Misc. Magic Mishaps
MUST HAVE KEEPER PRESENT AT ALL TIMES WHILE IN THIS SECTION

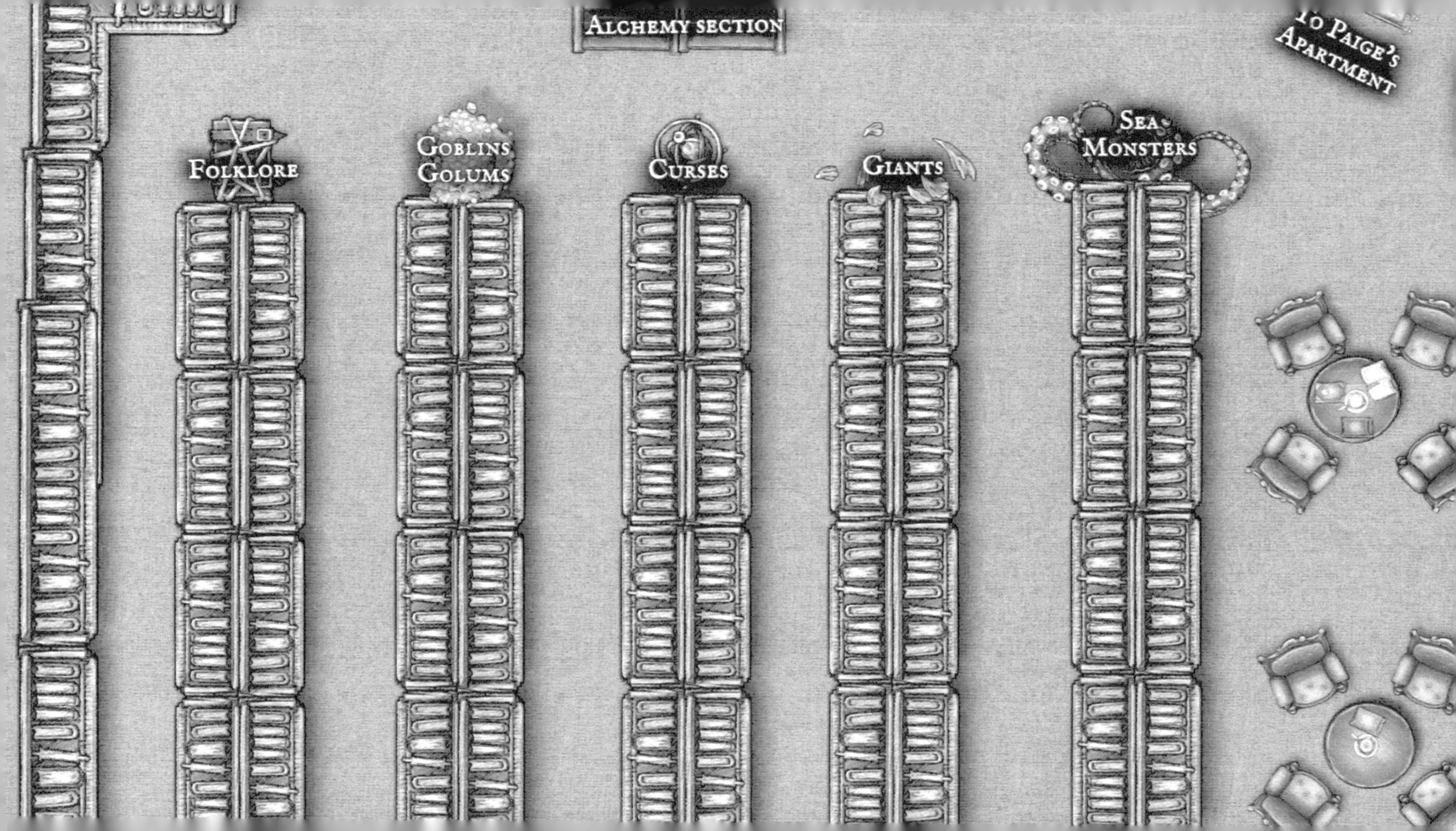
Alchemy section
To Paige's
Apartment
Folklore
Goblins
Golums
Curses
Giants
Sea
Monsters

1

ARIES

Drenched in warm Astronian sunlight, Paige presses her hands to my chest, her chestnut gaze earnest and full of determination. "Let's go take back your world, Your Highness. Then, we return to liberate mine."

I don't know what to say.

My mind is still reeling from everything that happened inside the Athenaeum, and my dragon is still furious with me for not burning Constantine to the ground before we came through that portal.

To be fair, Paige was right. Fire and libraries don't go well together, and had I unleashed my dragon's breath against the monster who drove us out and nearly killed us in the process, I would've burned the entire place to ash, books included.

Losing books is one thing, but the lives contained inside them are another. Every volume inside the Athenaeum contains an entire realm's story. My world is one of them.

Astronia.

We've arrived just south of the valley where the village is nestled with the castle on the hill above it. The forest at our backs obscures the view of both, but I'd know this spot anywhere. It's a place I used to come often just to get away from palace life for a little while.

I look out at the rolling hills below that give way to mountains in the distance. So much green. Fresh air. And not a single smog-producing car contraption in sight. Getting sucked into the Earth realm was an adventure unlike any other. And while falling for Paige is something I'll never regret, it's damn good to be home.

The relief builds inside me until my dragon wants to let out a roar. I resist the urge to let my wings out. I want to leap into the air and fly and scout.

Scout.

The war.

The horde.

My stomach drops as I remember what I read about what's become of my home in my absence. According to the last entry in my book, war is pressing down upon my world. And without me here to stop it, the horde of evil orcs wins.

Have I come back in time?

Or is it already too late?

"Aries?" Paige presses. "You okay?"

I glance back at the others and realize they're all watching me warily now. For the first time since I met the guardians of the Athenaeum, Keepers as they call themselves, they are looking to me for the answers. Blossom, Mag, the four gnomes—even Bingo—are all out of their element here.

"It's not usually this quiet," I say at last.

Where are the patrols? This hillside is carefully guarded. Or it was. Before…

"Really?" Paige frowns as she, too, looks out at the beautiful view spread before us. "It seems like a pretty remote spot."

I shake my head. "The village is not far through these trees.

We patrol this area regularly. Someone should have noticed us out here by now."

Instantly, Blossom, a fierce unicorn shifter and possibly the last of her kind, looks around warily, clearly picking up on my stiffening posture. Her stark white hair billows as she surveys our surroundings.

"Do you think something's happened to the guards?" Paige asks, moving over to be closer to the gnomes—Ted, Zed, Ned, and Fred. Kitty, their raccoon, paws the ground nervously.

"I don't know."

My gaze falls on Bingo, a fierce and growly hellhound who serves as one of the Athenaeum's protectors.

Used to serve.

Bingo meets my gaze and huffs through his large nostrils.

He's wary too.

"Something's not right," I say as the wind picks up, rustling through the trees. I turn toward it, reaching out with my dragon's senses.

The scent of smoke—and beneath it, death—hits me, and I stiffen, scanning the horizon for different reasons now. "I fear I've been gone too long. We need to get to the castle."

"Lead the way, Your Highness," Mag says to me.

I make a face, but hand in hand with Paige, I start walking away from the cliffside. It doesn't sit well with me for my friends to call me that, which is strange since I was born and raised to be king one day, ruling beside my mate. I knew this, and I accepted it—and more, I wanted it.

Unlike my brother.

Leo is a second-born prince through and through. If he's been forced to take the crown in my absence, he is not going to be happy. He was more than satisfied to leave the throne for me and keep all the freedom and adventure for himself. His words, not mine. Then again, if there were a dragon king sitting on the

Astronian throne, the future wouldn't look so bleak for my people.

I think of the book Paige is carrying. The one that tells the story of my world and its people—and me. I wonder if the story has changed at all now that I've returned. It's tempting to ask her to stop and show it to me. But if I'm going to save my world, I must join the fight, not read about it.

The farther we walk, the louder my dragon becomes in my head, urging me to unleash my wings and take to the skies, to reclaim them as his own. But if my kingdom is under attack, the last thing I want to do is to be spotted—or worse, alert the enemy to the location of the others. Mag and Blossom are formidable warriors, but we can't handle an entire horde of orcs by ourselves. Not after the battle we just fought to get here.

Beside me, Paige is quiet. Through our bond, I can feel her emotions swirling with both relief and worry. The adrenaline has worn off, and the reality of what we've been through has started to settle in. The gnomes are silent, forgoing their usual chattiness as we march. Even Blossom and Mag are beginning to show signs of exhaustion. Constantine's creatures were relentless.

We're lucky to be alive.

I just hope I can say the same for my own family.

"Are you nervous?" Paige whispers to me as we near the edge of the trees.

"I'm relieved to be back," I say, not sure how to put into words everything running through me just now. "To help them fight if needed."

She squeezes my hand, lowering her voice to a whisper. "I get that. I don't mean about the orcs. I meant about seeing your family."

I glance back and note that Mag and Blossom have put some distance between us as they guard our rear. Bingo has disappeared, but I can scent him close by in the trees, scouting.

I glance at Paige again, unwilling to admit that nervous doesn't begin to cover it. "I suppose how long I've been away will play a role, especially if Leo has ascended the throne in my absence."

Saying the words aloud makes my gut twist. If it's already done, there will be no way to undo it. And my future will have changed forever.

"No matter what, Aries, you have me."

I lean over and kiss Paige's temple. "That will always be enough," I tell her.

"Besides," she adds, "that would only happen if Leo's found his mate, right?"

"True. And Leo never wanted the throne." I snort before adding, "But he wouldn't mind searching through all the potential mates in this kingdom to fulfill his duties."

Paige chuckles.

"Sounds like he's someone Mag might get along with," Blossom calls out.

"Who doesn't get along with me?" Mag asks.

Blossom groans, and I don't have to turn around to know she's likely rolling her eyes.

We ascend the final hill, and I come to an abrupt halt. Beside me, Paige gasps. The others come up behind us. One of the gnomes grabs my leg for support. I don't look down to see who it is.

"Who did this?" Mag asks, quiet rage lacing his words.

I don't answer, unable to look away from the village nestled in the valley below the castle. While my castle appears intact and unharmed, the entire village is scorched and crumbling.

"What happened?" Blossom asks.

"Orcs," Paige answers grimly.

All eyes swing to me.

My hands curl into fists as the need for vengeance nearly takes me over. "The war has begun."

Or it's already over.

With my blood churning, I race down the hill to the gates of the city. The road is barricaded from the outside, but it's an easy task to toss aside enough of the rubble to gain access. The gates themselves are burnt and broken, and the guardhouses are empty.

The others are right behind me as we pass through them into the city.

We walk silently, and I remain watchful for some sign of danger. But nothing moves or comes to greet us, least of all the people who lived here.

"Where is everyone?" Blossom asks in a hushed tone.

I don't answer.

"Hopefully, they got out," Paige says, the words strained with worry—and fear.

I look over, wanting to comfort or reassure her, especially after what we've just gone through. I note the blood on her clothes and the tear in her shirt. Blossom is equally as disheveled. Mag's flesh has already turned to stone, and I know he's bracing himself for a threat as I am.

"Please tell me we didn't leave one battle behind only to have to fight another," Blossom says.

Paige offers her an apologetic look. "Aries' homeland has been attacked by an army of orcs in his absence."

"You're serious?" Blossom glares at her. "You really conjured a portal straight into a war? Are you for real right now?"

"It's why we've been trying to get back here," Paige tells her. "I'm sorry, but Aries' people need him. And us."

"Girl, you are so lucky I love to kill things," Blossom says.

Paige smiles. "I love that about you."

"Me too," Mag adds.

Blossom rolls her eyes. "You're such a kiss ass," she tells him.

"I hope you mean that literally," Mag tosses back with a wink.

Blossom groans, but her irritation is gone, and we all go back to searching for signs of life.

When we come to the alehouse, I veer off and walk to the door. It's shut but unlocked and pushes open easily at my touch. I peer into the shadowy interior and find it empty. There are a few plates of aged food sitting out as if the customers left in a hurry. I scent nothing recent in terms of visitors.

Turning away, I resume our trek, stopping to check several more homes and businesses.

All empty.

My worry grows even as I tell myself it's better to find the place empty than full of bodies.

"This ghost town doesn't have any real ghosts at least," Mag says at last.

I glare at him. One of the books that we explored in our fruitless venture to save Hoc, Paige's adoptive father, had been a literal ghost town. The ghosts in residence hadn't been the most pleasant.

Blossom smacks Mag.

"I was just trying to lighten the mood," he protests.

"Maybe learn to read the room?" Paige suggests.

Mag grimaces. "I didn't mean to offend."

"Let's just get to the castle," I manage.

We hurry through the eerily silent village and up the winding path toward the castle. It looms above us at the top of the valley, and as we near it, I sense movement.

Relief washes over me as a castle guard comes into view. I don't recognize him, but that doesn't mean much. My personal interactions only ever extended to the officers and my own personal guard. This man is neither.

He appears unharmed and fully alert in his royal uniform,

though I note the battle armor he wears even in broad daylight at the castle gates.

"Halt! Identify yourselves," the guard demands.

The others stop as a dozen spears are aimed in our direction.

I step forward, lifting my head high so they can see me clearly. "I am Aries Nemos, heir to the throne of Astronia, defender of this land, and your future king."

He glances at my clothing, which is much different than the styles of this world, and confusion mars his features. But when he sees my face, his eyes widen in recognition, and he bows.

"Your Highness." He motions to the other guards. "Lower your weapons!"

They quickly do as he says and bow their heads.

A moment later, the iron gate at his back opens and we're ushered through.

"Come," I say to the others, grabbing Paige's hand tightly.

The guards remain with heads bowed as we pass. No one comments on my attire that they surely think bizarre. Not to mention the other creatures I've brought with me. We make a motley crew, especially since Mag is still a walking stone gargoyle, but I wouldn't exchange any of them for the world.

Inside the castle walls, nearly every available space is cramped with villagers. They line the walls and crowd into the alleyways between the royal shops, some with tents erected as if they've claimed the cobblestones as their own.

Despite the masses, my attention is drawn to the obvious pageantry going on inside the castle itself. Trumpets are blaring. Banners soar, decorated in the royal colors and crest. Something important is going on.

I start forward anxiously.

"What's the celebration?" Paige asks one of the villagers.

"The royal wedding, of course," the elderly woman replies gaily.

Paige and I exchange a glance, and then I'm hurrying through the crowd.

I lead the way into the castle and straight to the throne room with the others close on our heels. Guards pull the doors open for us, each one lowering their heads in recognition once they spot me.

Inside, I come to a stop as I sweep the large room and the absurd number of people in it.

High vaulted ceilings cause the hum of voices to echo loudly. Massive columns, intricately carved with images of dragons, are wrapped in gold and silver ribbons. Large tapestries, each one depicting battles and dragons, hang between large arched windows.

I look past all the decorations, my heart thudding wildly.

At the end of the aisle, my mother stands on the raised platform in front of the double emerald thrones meant for the two rulers of Astronia. On either side of the thrones are large twin statues of dragons in smooth marble, their ruby eyes fixed on the crowd.

But I can't look away from the couple standing before my mother. The male is my height, but where I have the muscles, he is lean and lithe. Even if I didn't know my brother's figure, I'd know him by his dress. The overdone finery is typical for an event such as this, but even if it weren't, Leo has always preferred the extravagant.

Beside him is a woman dressed in white and heavily veiled.

This isn't any wedding.

This is my brother's wedding.

And a coronation.

"Uh-oh," Mag says loudly.

Every single guest turns to see the commotion we've caused.

"What is this interruption?" my mother declares loudly before her gaze finally lands on me. Her eyes widen, and the color drains from her face, but she recovers the next moment. "Aries! You have returned!"

The crowd begins to murmur, but my mother waves away the people. "This ceremony is concluded until further notice," she announces. "You may exit immediately."

The guards shoo the guests toward the doors still open behind us, and people begin to file past us in droves.

My mother rushes between Leo and his *bride? Wife?* Is the wedding over? Did we miss it? She practically shoves them aside in her haste down the aisle to where I stand.

Leo hurries behind Mother. "Aries, it is so good—"

"What is all of this?" the bride screeches.

Her gown is more extravagant than any I've ever seen with enough layers and lace that I'm not sure how she's able to walk beneath the weight of it. She does her best to hurry up the aisle behind Leo, and I can't help but think she looks familiar. But then my mother steps in, blocking my view.

"Aries, it's really you," my mother breathes as she reaches me. She grabs me and pulls me into a tight hug. "I can't believe it. I thought you… but no, I never lost hope."

I wrap my arms around her, relief and joy filling me. Before I left, my mother had been driving me crazy with her matchmaking, but now, I'm simply grateful to find her alive and well.

"I'm home, Mother."

When she releases me, her eyes are watery though she manages to hold back actual tears. Ever the well-mannered royal. "Where have you been?" she asks.

"I was called away," I say, reaching for Paige's hand.

My mother steps back, eyeing us both with a new expression. I can see the questions forming, but she doesn't get to ask a single one before Leo is shoving his way forward and grasping me in a quick hug.

"Right on time," he tells me with a grin. And then to my mother, he adds, "The wedding is off now, is it not?"

Relief shudders through me. We're just in time then.

Behind Leo, through her veil, I can see the bride's expression become horrified. "You can't—"

"Aries has returned, so there is no need for Leo to marry, especially not to a woman who is not his mate," my mother says firmly. The queen turns to the wide-eyed bride, whom I finally begin to realize is familiar to me. "I am sorry, Esma, but you know we all had reservations about this arrangement considering Leo wouldn't have been able to ensure the dragon line continued without his fated mate."

Esma, a flamingo shifter who'd not-so-subtly let her interest in me be known, rips her veil back, glaring.

"Hello, Esma," I say as politely as I can.

Beside me, Paige tenses.

Esma gives me a once-over and then lifts her chin with renewed determination. "Well, then, Aries needs to be wed if the crown is to go to him, and since I'm already dressed for the occasion—"

"That won't be necessary. I have my mate," I say.

My mother's expression fills with happiness, but the flamingo shifter's eyes narrow. Her pinched lips and her wrinkled nose make her appear bird-like—and scheming.

"That's outrageous," Esma declares though no one acknowledges her.

"Oh, thank goodness," Leo exclaims. He glances from Paige to Blossom and even to Mag before asking, "Which one is your mate?"

I shake my head. As if our tightly joined hands didn't give it away.

Paige shyly steps forward, but she lifts her chin and smiles. "That would be me."

Leo grabs her free hand and sinks to his knees. "You have saved my life, sweetheart."

I roll my eyes, and Blossom snickers, clearly entertained by Leo's dramatics.

"I owe you a life debt," Leo continues, "for saving me from that woman." He jabs his thumb at Esma, who looks ready to explode with fury.

"Excuse me. This is your mate?" Esma shrieks. "This… this… this mouse of a woman?"

Paige stiffens.

I squeeze her hand, speaking up quickly. "I assure you my mate is no mouse."

Esma's eyes narrow, and I can see she's not going to let this go. "What is she then?" Esma demands. "Not another dragon, or I would sense it."

"Aries has found his mate," my mother interrupts, her tone cool. "You know how important that is for the kingdom's future. Your service is appreciated, but you are no longer needed, Esma. The guards will escort you home."

Once more, Esma glowers at Paige before she all but stomps out of the throne room, her head jerking forward and back, making her look even more like a bird than normal.

"Fucking flamingos," Mag mutters.

Leo snorts. "You have no idea."

Then he shudders, and that is all it takes for me to roar with laughter. I embrace my brother, clapping him on the back. I have not felt happier since, well, since the claiming bite.

"Mother, allow me to introduce you to Paige Murphy, my mate and Astronia's new queen. Paige, this is my mother, Dorthea Nemos, Astronia's ruling queen."

I fall silent, my heart nearly beating out of my chest. Will my mother approve of a mate from a far-off world? One who is not a shifter and not one of us? Will she say something to alienate Paige when we need to be united? My mother is a good woman, but she is also set in her ways and opinionated, and if she agreed to have Leo marry Esma despite what that meant for our dragon line, then my mother is quite desperate.

"It is so nice to meet you," Paige says warmly.

I can sense some nerves through our bond, but she's also… hopeful.

My mother takes Paige's hands in hers and looks her up and down. "It is very nice to meet you, Paige Murphy, though you are not yet Astronia's queen."

Paige's smile falters.

"But you will be soon enough," my mother finishes, her smile radiant and welcoming. "We have a kingdom to save."

2

PAIGE

Despite the queen's warm welcome, my emotions churn into a swirling mess as she talks. I do my best to keep up with everything she's saying about finding me some clothes before giving me a proper introduction to the kingdom and something about a council who still needs to approve of it all. Between the adrenaline from fighting Constantine and then the high of controlling my powers and creating the portal that brought us here, I'm nearing exhaustion. But even more than sleep, I need food.

With the queen still talking, my stomach growls so loudly that everyone turns to look.

Heat floods my cheeks. "Sorry," I mumble.

"Your stomach is just saying what we're all thinking," Blossom says with a snort.

"There was to be a feast after the wedding," Aries' mother says with zero trace of judgment. "I will see to it that the villagers are all still fed, and then we can all go eat dinner together privately."

Her gaze shifts from Aries back to me and then Blossom and

Mag and the gnomes. She seems surprised by the gnomes, but she smiles warmly at them. "Hello."

"Your Majesty." The gnomes all speak in unison and then nearly fall over, trying to bow at her feet.

The queen's smile is amused. "And you are?"

The gnomes speak up one at a time, their chests puffing up proudly as they identify themselves.

"I'm Ted."

"I'm Zed."

"I'm Ned."

"And I'm Fred." Kitty nudges Fred so hard he almost falls over. "And this is Kitty," he adds hastily.

"And Bingo," Ned pipes up. "He's our hellhound. But he only eats bad guys, so you don't have to worry about that."

"Just stop talking," Blossom mutters.

"A hellhound?" The queen's eyes widen, and she looks to Aries. "They are only myths."

Bingo growls at that, and the queen goes pale.

"This one is very much real," Aries says.

"And harmless," I add with a pointed look at the beast.

He shuts up.

The queen takes a steadying breath, and her composure instantly returns. "I'll go speak to the staff about feeding the guests and return in a moment." She glances at Blossom and Mag and adds, "I look forward to getting to know you all."

Then she walks away. No, *walks* isn't the word for it. Glides. Waltzes. She probably has more grace in her pinky than I have in my entire body.

Ugh.

I'm nothing like her or even Esma, the horrid woman Leo would have married if we hadn't crashed the wedding. I hope Aries doesn't regret—

He eyes me, giving me a sexy crooked grin that sends a jolt

straight through me. He's mine, and I am his. We don't have to be married for that to be true.

He's my fated mate. Already claimed, in fact, so there's no going back.

"We like her," Ted declares when the queen is gone.

"She said we're going to have a feast," Ned adds excitedly.

"We're going to eat like kings," Fred declares.

Zed rubs his hands together. "Do you think she has any candy?"

I chuckle. Somehow, I doubt this world has the treats they're used to, but I don't tell them that.

"Just please be on your best behavior," I warn them.

Leo turns to me. "Paige, I mean it, I cannot begin to tell you how thankful I am that you are here. You truly saved me from a fate worse than death."

Aries snorts. "You are freed up to find your own fated mate now."

"Eventually." Leo winks. "But for now, I can go back to being a second-born prince and, more importantly, fiancé-free." He brightens as he turns to Blossom.

Uh oh. I recognize that look.

"And you are? Besides gorgeous, that is," Leo says.

"I'm Blossom," she says, smirking.

"Blossom. Beautiful name. Unicorn shifter, right?"

"How did you know?" she asks, immediately suspicious.

"Dragon senses," Leo tells her confidently. "You certainly are one of a kind."

Mag clears his throat. "Sounds to me like Astronia has no need of a second-born prince," he growls.

Leo glances from the unicorn shifter to the gargoyle and holds up his hands. "My apologies. I didn't realize… I meant no offense. The lovely Blossom is with the clearly capable…?"

"Mag," hc grunts.

"Mag. A pleasure to meet you, and I mean that. I don't know

what circumstances brought you all together, but if you had a hand in bringing my brother home, then I'm grateful."

"Someone had to watch his back," Mag says with a shrug.

"Then I thank you sincerely from the bottom of my heart. I wasn't there, and you kept him safe. That means everything." Leo clasps Mag's hand, and I watch as the gargoyle relaxes a bit.

Aries leans down close to my ear. "Mag has always reminded me of Leo," he whispers in my ear. "I knew that either meant they would be the best of friends or mortal enemies."

"Let's hope for friendship," I whisper back.

He grins.

I can sense his elation through our bond. He's glad to be home even if it means facing the danger at his doorstep.

The queen returns, her heels clicking over the marble floors. She looks every inch a queen, too. Her gown is a mix of the Medieval and Regency eras. It's beautiful, but it's not something I would've ever thought to wear even as a Halloween costume. Will I have to wear something like that flamingo woman did when Aries and I get married?

"Here we are," the queen says as she bends down and hands a basket filled with cookies and biscuits to Zed and Ned. "I thought you might like a little treat to tide you over until dinner."

The gnomes all chatter and cheer for the unexpected food. I watch with amusement, knowing full well that woman just sealed her place in their hearts forever.

"It's not exactly Sour Patch, but it's pretty good," Zed comments around a mouthful of cookie.

"What is a sour patch?" the queen asks.

Blossom and Mag both grin.

"A sugary substance with a sourness that will make your lips pucker," Aries explains.

"And this is considered tasty?" the queen asks, blinking.

Blossom snorts. "It is to them."

"I apologize. I didn't get your name," the queen says to her.

Blossom straightens, her smile suddenly gone. "I'm Blossom; this is Mag," she says, hooking her thumb at the gargoyle.

"I see. It's a pleasure to meet you all," the queen says.

The gnomes all finish their treat and shove at each other as they go back for seconds. The queen snatches the basket only to realize it's already empty.

"My goodness," she says. "You must have been starving. Did they not feed you in your own lands?"

"Not nearly enough," Ted says, batting his eyes at the queen and stealing pointed glances at me.

I shake my head, not willing to take the bait.

"Come with me, and I'll get you something more while we wait," she tells them patiently. "Dinner will be ready shortly, and then we can talk more," she says to the rest of us before leading the gnomes out.

When they're gone, Aries wraps his arm around me, and I lean against him, drawing strength from him. I need him to ground me because, if not, I'm afraid I'll fall apart.

Leo, Mag, and Blossom have shifted to the side, talking and laughing quietly. Bingo has wandered closer, sniffing at Leo, who pats his head and then laughs at something Mag said. When he moves his hand away, Bingo growls, and Leo laughs again and scratches behind Bingo's ear.

Aries nudges me. "How are you holding up?"

"I'm fine," I assure him.

His brow lifts at that. "I'm not sure I believe you, but we'll likely need to have dinner with my mother before we can get away to talk."

"We're alive and safe," I tell him. "And your throne still belongs to you. For now, that's all that matters."

He kisses me quickly, and we move over to join the others.

"You can lift something called a… car?" Leo is asking Mag. "Is it heavy?"

Blossom laughs, and Mag glares at her.

"Yes," Mag says at the same time Blossom says, "At least as heavy as a boulder."

Mag scowls. "More like a small house."

"And you can do that in this form or only when you become the stone monster?" Leo asks.

"In either form," Mag says haughtily. "And the term is gargoyle, not stone monster."

"I don't know. You can be a stone monster all right," Blossom says.

"I would love to see it," Leo says, eyes gleaming with the challenge.

Aries claps Leo's back. "We can hit the training ring soon. We'll see if you kept up with your training in my absence."

A shadow passes over Leo's expression, but he blinks it away. "I'd say my chances are better than ever now that Aries has gone soft for a mate." He winks at me adding, "At least, he's no longer my competition. Unless, of course, Paige is open to convincing…"

Aries growls and steps toward Leo, eyes narrowed. "Paige is mine."

"Whoa, kidding." Leo throws his hands up. "I meant no harm."

Aries continues to glare, so I tug him back.

"Forgive Aries," Mag says. "He's a little on edge. We all are."

Mag and Aries share a look, and suddenly, all the amusement is gone as we all remember what we went through to get out of the library. And who we left behind in our place.

"Did something happen on your journey here?" Leo asks.

I don't answer except to glance at Aries. There are parts of the story I'm not sure I'm ready to voice aloud. Not even to my friends.

"Paige's world is very different," Aries says, and I shoot him a grateful look. "There were some who made our exit difficult. We're just tired from the journey."

Leo frowns. I can see the questions forming, but he doesn't ask them.

"Of course," he says, clapping Aries on the back. "I'm just glad you're home now. Astronia needs its rightful king to defeat the horde once and for all."

"We saw the village on our way in," Aries says quietly. Leo's expression darkens again, and Aries matches it. "Tell me what happened."

Leo glances at the rest of us then back to his brother. It's clear there are things he wants to share privately.

"Go," I say, ushering Aries away. "I could use a minute."

Aries nods slowly, though I can tell he doesn't want to exclude me.

"Go catch up with your brother," I say when he doesn't move.

"Fine, but I'll be right over here if you need me," Aries says.

"Come. Walk with me a moment." Leo leads Aries away. I watch them go, their heads bent close together as they talk quietly. Bingo follows, stopping to sniff here and there.

Mag and Blossom remain beside me.

"You okay?" Blossom asks quietly.

"Define okay," I say with a sigh.

"We're alive," Mag puts in. "That's a start."

"What's the plan?" Blossom asks. She glances from me to Mag as she adds, "Constantine is going to destroy that place if we let him."

"He won't," I say with way more confidence than I feel. "But Aries' world is in danger because of what I did by conjuring him that day. I owe it to him—to all of them—to help defend against the orcs."

Blossom doesn't say anything. She and Mag exchange a look.

"You don't have to fight," I tell them both. "This isn't your war, so I understand—"

"Aries fought for us," Mag says firmly. "I'll do the same for him."

Blossom nods, determination in her eyes. "Mag is right. We'll fight here, and when it's done, we'll deal with Constantine for good."

"Thanks," I tell them gratefully. "It means a lot to have you both by my side through all of this."

"We aren't going anywhere," Blossom says firmly. "Besides, you're our secret weapon now, Miss I-can-conjure-portals-at-will." She hip-bumps me. "That was kind of amazing."

"Thanks."

"At least, we know we can get back when we're ready to deal with him," Mag says.

Blossom nods. "I can't wait to see what else you have up your sleeve."

"Constantine won't know what hit him," Mag adds, eyes gleaming.

"Right," I say, forcing a smile.

Conjuring a portal to get us back into the library is one thing. What we'll do once we get there is another problem entirely. The last glimpse I had of the library was one full of dark, violent creatures bent on destroying us all. Creatures that are undoubtedly ready and waiting to try again should we return. I'm not sure my particular skillset helps us avoid that fate. But Blossom and Mag look at me with such belief that I can't bring myself to tell them I have no idea how to actually defeat the monster we fled from—which may very well mean the world as we know it will someday belong to him. Or worse, cease to exist at all.

3

ARIES

Leo fills me in on the horde's invasion which apparently began shortly after I left. I'm grateful he does so away from the others because the outlook is bleak. In the absence of ruling dragon mates on our throne, the orcs have become increasingly brave. By the time Leo has caught me up on the latest attack—the one that drove the villagers here to the castle—I'm feeling the weight of it all bearing down on my shoulders.

There's so much at stake here. Every Astronian life poised beneath the blade's edge. Now that I'm home, it's up to me to lead us all to safety—except I've just come from a failed battle. I can't bring myself to tell Leo that part, so I evade his questions about my time in Paige's world, turning the subject back to our own at every turn.

Across the room, a maid enters and approaches us. "Dinner, Your Highnesses." She drops into a curtsy. "If you'll follow me, the queen and her new, um, friends will meet you there."

Paige quirks a brow. "The gnomes?"

I shrug. "I guess."

We're escorted to the family dining room where memories

wash over me. As always, without my father, it feels a bit empty—despite the extra people here. Another table has been brought in along with extra chairs to accommodate us all. As she has done since my father died, my mother sits at the head of the table. Once I am crowned, that will become my seat.

A reality that is speeding ever closer now that Paige is here.

I take the seat at my mother's right hand but not before holding the chair beside mine for Paige to sit. Leo settles across from me, and the others fill in around us. The gnomes are already seated at the opposite end, their plates laden with biscuits and desserts. Their shirts too.

With a rueful smile, my gaze shifts to the food. There is wild boar and pheasant, no doubt roasted to perfection. And seafood as well, clearly dragon-fire grilled, which leaves a nice, smoky taste. Likewise, the vegetables, different from those back in the library, are fire-roasted. There are rolls made from the same dough as the cookies my mother gave to the gnomes. Doubtless, there are even more desserts waiting once we finish with the main course.

"This looks delicious," Paige says.

"Definitely better than microwave dinners," Blossom adds.

"What's a microwave?" Leo asks.

Blossom merely shakes her head.

"A magical oven that zaps food to make it hot," Mag explains. Leo looks intrigued before Mag adds, "and zaps the flavor too."

"Ah."

"Please, eat your fill," my mother says.

It is only after we have started to eat with the others murmuring how delicious the fare is that my mother fixes me with a look.

"What is it?" I ask when she doesn't say anything.

She hesitates, glancing at the others. "Nothing. We'll talk later."

"Whatever you have to say, you can do so in front of them," I tell her. "They have saved my life more than once. I trust them implicitly."

"In that case," she says softly despite the sternness in her expression, "you should be made aware of all that has gone on in the months you were gone."

I choke on my ale. "Wait. Months?" I echo.

"It's been almost three moon cycles," Leo supplies, his brows knitting.

"You didn't tell me that," I say, replaying my conversation with him from earlier. But now it makes sense. The horde couldn't have organized in mere days. They've had months to plan, prepare, and finally, to act.

Still… it feels impossible.

I've only been gone a few weeks, according to the Athenaeum's time.

"I don't understand. Was it not the same amount of time where you were?" my mother asks, frowning.

"It seems not," I say tightly. My mother starts to respond. "That's a story for another time," I add. "Let's focus on the horde for now."

"All right," she says slowly.

Paige reaches beneath the table to squeeze my knee. I place my hand on top of hers, doing my best to keep my emotions even.

"So, Leo has told you of the attacks on the villages along the border," my mother continues.

"Yes," I say, suddenly no longer hungry.

A quick glance reveals Mag and Blossom also abandoning their food as they listen intently.

"Is that why the castle is so crowded?" Paige asks.

My mother nods. "The horde attacked without warning. None of our scouts or soldiers saw it coming. One day, they were unorganized, unprepared, and the next—" She breaks off and changes direction. "When the villages along the border fell so swiftly, our soldiers scrambled to drive the enemy back again. The horde used our distraction to attack Havenford itself a fortnight ago. We brought all survivors inside the castle walls." Her expression becomes strained. "Though I'm not sure how long we can sustain such a population."

"The horde were never strong enough for this," I say, my hand curling into a fist where it rests on the table. "They shouldn't be this strong now."

"Our strength has always come from two ruling mates. The horde senses our weakness," my mother says.

"Does having a mated king on the throne really make the kingdom so much stronger?" Paige asks.

"Astronia has lasted eons because of the magic of the dragon line that rules it," my mother tells her. "When the goddess created this world, she entrusted it to the Nemos dragon line, promising to imbue it with her magic and her strength so long as they dedicated their lives to protect it from those who would hurt and destroy.

"In past centuries, the horde tested that magic by attacking. They were swiftly defeated every time. Eventually, they realized that the goddess spoke true and they would never be a match for us. Now… the horde knows our family's magic has been weakening since my husband died."

My mother glances at me. There's no blame or even disappointment in her words, but I feel a pang of guilt all the same. I've taken too long to ascend, and now, our people are paying with their lives.

Her grim expression lightens a little as she adds, "We will show them the full strength of our dragon king soon enough."

"All hail the king," Mag says with more sarcasm than he should.

I glare at him.

"We feared the worst with your disappearance," Leo says

quietly. "We thought maybe the horde had taken you, but when there was no ransom, no taunting… Some feared you had been killed."

"I am alive and ready to fight," I assure him, still not sure how to explain my sudden departure—or the fact that we left behind an enemy even more powerful and deadly than the orcs. "How many have we lost?"

"The first two villages were completely wiped out," Leo says. "Our people just weren't prepared. Since then, we've managed to relocate civilians from the outlying towns to the larger ones with more defensive structures in place. Our numbers are holding."

He doesn't have to add *for now*.

"In between battles, we planned the wedding between Leo and Esma," my mother adds tightly.

It's clear she wasn't thrilled about the prospect of welcoming Esma into the family. I can't blame her.

"But would that have returned your dragon magic?" Paige asks, concern pinching her brow.

"It was a Band-aid at best," Leo says. "Mostly because Esma isn't my mate—in case you couldn't tell." He winks, but his grin vanishes quickly as he adds, "It was a gamble whether an unmated pair would have the same effect on our magic, but the council agreed that we had no choice but to try."

"I take it you haven't had the chance to be paraded past all of the beautiful maidens yet, then," I tease.

"Oh, Mother did her best, believe me." Leo rubs his hands together with glee. "Though, now that I am free, I think I would appreciate that parade very much."

Bingo sits up from his place on the rug and snarls.

"Calm down, Bingo," Paige says.

Leo turns toward the large black hound. "What's wrong? Do you want to join me for the parade?"

"I think he just wants to make sure you don't bring home any more flamingos," Mag puts in.

"No more flamingos, I swear it," Leo vows, his hand held up in oath.

My mother rolls her eyes and sighs, but even she is smiling as the rest of us join in the laughter.

Bingo seems a bit mollified, especially as Leo starts to feed him slivers of pheasant from his plate.

"So, if I have this straight," Blossom says to me, "Your kingdom is jointly ruled?"

I nod. "Precisely."

"By a dragon and his mate," she continues.

"Well, the dragon could be a female," I say, "but in recent generations, the dragon who has ruled has always been a son. Dragons tend to have more sons than daughters."

"I am not a dragon," my mother explains. "I am a fae, but as I was my husband's fated mate, I ruled as his equal. And my children are both dragons."

"Equal opportunity monarchy, I like it." Blossom slowly nods and then winks at Paige. "Hear that, Paige? Your babies will all be dragons."

Paige's face flushes at that. Under the table, I find her hand and squeeze.

"I always knew you would go places, kid, but to become a full-blown queen? That's impressive," Mag says.

"I have long waited to pass on my crown," my mother says. She turns to Paige, adding, "I look forward to having you as a new member of our family."

"Thank you." Paige's cheeks turn pink again. "Does that mean… well, it sounds like we need to be married as soon as possible in order to restore the kingdom's magic."

"It would be ideal," my mother agrees. Her expression is troubled now, and I tense at the look she and Leo share.

"What is it?" I ask.

"If you will forgive me, Paige," my mother says, sidestepping my question with all the grace of a monarch, "I cannot quite tell what form of creature you are. I can sense you are powerful, and… Forgive me. I should not have asked. It is rude."

"It's only natural to be curious about the woman who is the fated mate of your son," Paige says. "You don't need to apologize. There's nothing to forgive. I'm…" She hesitates.

"She's a mage," I supply, understanding her reluctance to claim that title.

Paige winces, clearly not yet comfortable with that title.

"A mage! That will help immensely with our defenses," my mother says.

"I will help where I can," Paige says warily.

"Your magic will be more than able to help our soldiers on the battlefield," I assure her.

"I didn't mean to suggest that you put her on the front lines. Aries, if she is harmed—" my mother starts.

"She won't be," I say simply, proudly. "She has already fought with us and protected us truer than any soldier. Her magic is powerful. *She* is powerful."

Paige offers a weak smile. "Thank you."

"I'll watch her back," Blossom cuts in.

"And I'll watch both of their backs," Mag adds.

Bingo growls.

"Do you want to fight?" I ask Bingo.

The hound nods.

"We'll fight too," Zed adds from the far end of the table.

Everyone looks over, surprised. Up until now, they'd ignored the conversation in favor of the food. Mostly, the sweet potato pies as evidenced by so much of it on their faces.

"You'll do no such thing." My mother gasps at them. "You all are very brave, to be sure, but—"

"We have Kitty," Ned tells her, petting the raccoon.

“And these,” Fred adds, pulling his tiny dagger out of its holster.

“We know how to fight,” Zed adds defensively.

“We can discuss that later,” I say, hoping to diffuse a full argument.

The gnomes are skilled warriors in their own right, but I’m not sure arguing with the queen of Astronia at her own table is the way to prove it.

Instead, I change the subject in a direction I know will distract us all—and save my questions for the right moment. “Leo, did I tell you Mag and I met a mermaid during my time away?”

“Mermaid?” Leo’s eyes light up.

“Three, actually.” I grin as Mag groans. “But I’ll let Mag tell it.”

4

ARIES

We talk and eat for another hour. As much as I want to discuss battle strategy and next steps in this war, I allow Leo and Mag to dominate much of the conversation, which means it's more lighthearted than informative. My mother talks to Paige as much as she does me, but none of those from the library mention where we came from, and we aren't asked any more about how we came to be together.

I don't wish to lie, exactly, but the stress in both Leo and my mother is evident. I won't burden them with news of more war and battle than they're already dealing with.

"Are you a princess in your homeland?" my mother asks Paige over dessert.

Paige stifles a laugh. "Ah, no."

"She had a leadership position," I cut in.

"Very good." This pleases my mother, although if she were to stop and wonder if that means Paige had been employed, she might not be quite so happy. "And you do want children?"

"Mother, please. The war is our focus now," I remind her.

"I do want children one day, yes," Paige says.

I'm surprised she doesn't blush again, but instead, she seems self-assured, which satisfies my dragon greatly. Especially thinking about the undertaking of impregnating her.

Paige squirms slightly, squeezing her legs together, and I can't stop smiling to myself at her arousal.

Thankfully, my mother being a fae means she most likely can't also smell that. However, Leo and Blossom both can, and I hope they are too distracted to notice.

"Is your family back in your world?" my mother continues.

I tense, wondering if I should interrupt the conversation, but Paige answers before I can figure out what to say.

"My father passed away recently. The rest of my family is here," she says, gesturing to everyone present with a wave of her hand.

My mother smiles at them all. "In that case, you are our family too."

Conversation shifts as the gnomes are caught feeding Kitty under the table. Blossom fusses while Leo laughs. Bingo growls, probably out of jealousy, so Mag tosses him a large bone from the center platter.

Amid the hum of voices, my mother stands.

"Walk with me?" she asks, gesturing toward the doors that lead to the small balcony outside.

I nod and touch Paige's shoulder. "I'll be right back."

She pats my hand. "I'll be fine here," she assures me.

I offer my mother my arm and escort her outside into the night. It's a relief, the fresh air on my face. We can't see much beyond the castle walls from our vantage point, and my dragon yearns to be set free to fly high above the clouds.

My mother says nothing, her hands gripping the banister.

"I know she isn't who you would have picked—" I begin.

"Aries." She clucks her tongue. "Claiming your mate was never about finding someone that I approve of or not." She turns to me with approval in her eyes. "The choice has always been yours, and she's more than enough."

"Then what's wrong? And don't tell me it's nothing. I can see it all over your face tonight."

She sighs. "While your father lived, we had peace. After that, I gave everything I could to hold onto that peace. It is my greatest disappointment that I could not…" She swallows hard before going on. "While I hope that you and Paige will restore that peace, for now, Astronia needs a much different queen than I can offer them. It does my heart well to hear she is a warrior."

I warm at the compliment, but it's not enough to distract me from whatever she's holding back. "But," I prompt.

"But the council may feel differently."

The council.

I should have guessed.

My father was the most democratic king of his line, and while the people loved him for it, the egotistical, privileged people he elevated to power cling to their titles and their tradition with an ever-tightening vise grip.

"What have they said?" I ask.

"Leo's arrangement with Esma was their idea," she admits, exhaustion creeping in now that we're alone and she's confiding. "And it wasn't a suggestion, either."

I frown. "You make it sound like they're the ones giving the orders now?"

She sighs, and in that sound is exhaustion—and defeat. "I couldn't hold them off any longer without risking the throne itself."

Shock then anger simmers in my blood. These men are meant to advise and advocate—not dictate to the crown. "Paige is my mate. I have already claimed her. They have no authority to oppose a rightful king and queen."

She looks ready to argue, but in the end, she merely says, "If there's anyone who can get through to them, it's you."

"Tomorrow," I say, thinking of Paige. "Tonight, my friends and I need rest. Our journey has not been an easy one."

“Of course, darling. I’m so glad you’re here.”

“As am I.”

I press a kiss to her cheek and return to the others. Paige looks exhausted. Blossom has her head propped on her hand, elbow on the table, and Mag is outright yawning.

“I think it’s time for us to be shown to our rooms,” I announce.

“I suppose you are right.” My brother stands and nods to a maid lingering near the wall. “We need… How many rooms?”

“The gnomes might get into mischief if they are in a room by themselves,” Paige says.

“Hey,” Ned protests.

“Mag and I will take them,” Blossom says. “And Bingo if he wants to come.”

“You don’t have to do that,” Paige tells her, stifling another yawn.

“If they get out of hand, I’ll find a dungeon to lock them in.” The gnomes protest, but Blossom ignores them, winking at Paige. “Just go enjoy some time with your dragon prince. And try to get some sleep.”

Bingo brushes against Leo’s legs on his way to the door.

“Until morning, then?” Leo asks.

I nod and clap his back before ushering Paige out of the room, confident that the maid can handle securing the others a guest room.

Paige leans against me as I lead her through the castle to my chambers. My body relaxes as we step over the threshold. The worries will still be there tomorrow. Tonight, Paige is home with me where she belongs.

The room is as I left it, and the familiarity is a balm, giving me a sense of home I didn’t know I needed.

“Wow.” Paige walks over to my canopy bed, spins around, holds out her arms, and flops back onto it. “So soft,” she murmurs.

I laugh, even as my dragon roars at me to take her here—in my bed.

I cross over to stand before her reclined form, noting her closed lids. So much for a christening of this mattress tonight.

"Do you want to at least change your clothes?" I ask.

She groans, peeling her lids open as she lifts onto her elbows to peer up at me. "A shower would be even better."

"That part I can do," I say, heading for the connected washroom. I start the hot water running and toss some oils and salts into it before returning to the bedroom.

"Your bath is running," I tell her. "As for the night clothes, I'll have to call for a maid."

"Why?"

"I'm afraid the wardrobe in this room doesn't have a proper lady's nightclothes."

"Good thing I'm not a proper lady," she snorts.

I shake my head. "You need something to sleep in," I counter.

She manages to arch a brow. "So my clothes were good enough for you, but I can't wear yours?"

I chuckle, recalling the gray sweatpants she sewed for me the night we met. They had been rather snug, and they never did hide my erections around her, which I think she approved of greatly.

With two long strides, I cross over to the wardrobe and remove one of my extra tunics. She doesn't need pants, and they wouldn't fit her anyway.

"I think this will make us even," I say. "Come on."

I lead her into the bathroom where she stares hungrily at the large tub already filled with hot water. "This bathroom puts mine to shame."

I smirk. "Finally, you're impressed."

She runs her gaze over my body. "Oh, I was already impressed, believe me."

I smirk. As much as her teasing turns me on, I know she'll appreciate a moment to clean up. "In that case, enjoy."

I leave the tunic next to her towel and return to the bedroom to wait.

A few minutes later, Paige re-emerges in nothing but a towel. My body reacts instantly, and she doesn't miss the evidence, her gaze dipping to where my erection presses against my pants.

"Bath is all yours," she says.

With a groan, I stride into the bathroom and run fresh water —cold.

When I emerge a few minutes later, Paige has tossed the towel aside and is sliding the tunic over her head. I pause in the doorway, my gaze roving over her body. The lush curves of her breasts, the perfect shape of her hips. Thighs that clench when I send her soaring. She shrugs into the clothing and turns, noticing me at last.

Before my thoughts can betray me, I tear my gaze away and cross to my armoire to pull on clothes of my own. Finally, I climb into bed with her. Immediately, she curls beside me, resting her head on my chest.

"Paige, I can't thank you enough for bringing me home."

"That was our original plan," she reminds me, lifting her head so she can grin down at me. "Before you-know-who ruined it."

The mood plummets at the reminder.

She's quiet, and I wonder if she's thinking of Hoc. His death is the reason she was promoted to Head Librarian and forced to stay in the library instead of returning here with me sooner. I don't blame her, though. I chose to stay too. And I wouldn't change it. She needed me. But I can't deny the relief I feel at being back here—together.

"We're safe here," I say though that's not exactly true with the horde at our borders.

"Yes," she murmurs. "For now…"

"I will handle the orcs. Now that we're here—"

"We will win the war. I'm certain of it," she agrees sleepily. "But..."

I wait, trying to understand why I sense so much fear through our bond.

Fear and anger.

"We'll have to go back and face Constantine eventually," she reminds me.

"Will we?" I ask, the words slipping out before I can stop them.

"Aries." Paige sits up, frowning down at me. "You can't be serious."

"Think about it," I say earnestly. "We have my book, which means he can't get to us. To you. What if we just left it at that?"

She sits up, her hair tumbling over her shoulders. "He's violating the library's most sacred purpose," she argues, her voice rising. "He's taking what he wants from each world those books contain and destroying lives in the process. Just like he did to my world all those years ago."

Her voice cracks, nearly breaking.

"Tell me what happened," I say. "When you were gone with Oliver."

She hesitates, her fear written across her expression now.

"Paige, whatever it is, we can face it. Together."

She finally nods. "In that portal, I saw my home. The world I was born in," she adds before I can ask the question. "I saw my parents. Our village. It was a whole life, and it was beautiful. Filled with love. And hope. And then Constantine came."

"You saw his destruction," I say grimly.

"Yes, but not just that. When he was finished destroying, I watched myself... recreate it."

"What do you mean?"

"Constantine said my magic was the stardust of creation itself. I didn't understand at first, but in that memory, I watched myself recreate everything about my world—everything but the people I loved within it."

I soften at the way her voice cracks with grief.

"I replaced every single home and hearth and blade of grass that had been there before. But I can't bring back people." Her grief turns to frustration as she says, "What good is all this power if I can't save anyone with it?"

"You've saved us all," I remind her. "You found a way to get us out before he could hurt anyone else."

"I couldn't save Hoc," she says sadly.

"Hoc did what he did to save *you*."

"Yeah," she whispers half-heartedly. "Maybe you're right." She looks up at me, eyes shining. "I still can't believe Constantine was always there. In the library. That he's been feeding on my magic all these years." Anguish contorts her expression. "It's my fault he's this strong now. It's my fault he—"

"Whoa, hold on. If you hadn't conjured me, I might never have found my way to you." Her glistening eyes find mine, hope shining in them like desperation. "I don't regret a single second of being with you, Paige. Constantine's actions are his responsibility, not yours. Don't lay blame where it's not deserved."

"I don't regret you either," she tells me. "But don't you understand why I have to go back and finish this?"

"Yes." I reach for her, pulling her into my arms and holding her tight—as if this moment of closeness might somehow protect her from the danger that waits for us down the line. "I do understand. I just want to protect you from being hurt again."

She nestles closer, but she doesn't give in. "I appreciate that, but we can't hide. Eventually, he'll become powerful enough that he won't need the book to portal here." She pauses and then says, "He'll come for me, Aries. I can't explain how I know it, but I do. He won't stop until he's drained me for good."

She's right, of course.

Doesn't mean I like it.

"I would never let that happen," I snarl, tightening my grip on her and shoving aside the thought of her being harmed. Exhaling, I add, "You're right. He must be stopped, and the library must be restored. But let's focus on one war at a time. If we don't, we risk yet another lost world and nothing left in either one to save."

5

PAIGE

Rivers of blood flow behind my eyelids until this beautiful land is painted with it. Though, I can't tell whether it's the army of orcs who stain the soil—or the army of Astronia's king. The uncertainty leaves me shaken, and I jolt awake.

Aries is deeply asleep, clearly unaffected through the mate bond. Our bodies are tangled around one another, so rather than wake him, I stay where I am and glance around his room, studying the private space of the dragon heir in the shadowy moonlight. His canopy bed is magnificent and *massive*. It's so big that I wonder if it could fit his entire shifted dragon on it. The dark wood is glorious, carved into repeating patterns that look like dragon scales. Even more impressive is how luxurious the mattress is. Just what one would expect for a pampered dragon prince. Silk sheets, plush velvet pillows, the works.

It makes me wonder what Leo's room looks like. Probably trimmed in lace and leather and diamond-studded pillowcases. The thought almost makes me snort out loud as I let my gaze drift.

Across the room, I spot a desk covered with scrolls, books,

and parchments. Aries is a scholar? Clearly, we still have a lot to learn about one another. Beside the door to the bathroom, a massive fireplace is cut out, built from gray stone. Above it, a variety of weapons are mounted on the wall.

I shiver, imagining Aries wielding those instruments of death against an orc army. It's not a welcome idea even if the detail work is beautiful with dragon wings carved into the cross guards.

My thoughts return to the conversation we had just before bed. As much as I hate it, Aries is right about taking some time before rushing back to face Constantine. Astronia needs us right now. And more than that, I need to figure out what else I can do with this newly discovered magic I possess. Creating something from nothing—even something as big as a world—won't stop Constantine from consuming the magic I'll expel to do it. Even with the revelation of what I am and the magic I possess, I'm not sure it's enough to stop him or take back control of the library.

With too many questions and not enough answers, I snuggle close to Aries. In his sleep, he cradles me closer. Eventually, his warm embrace quiets my mind, and I slip back into sleep, dreamless this time.

When I wake again, I'm in bed alone. There's a handwritten note on the nightstand beside me.

Training with Leo. See you at lunch.

I smile, not at all feeling left out.

No, wait. Actually, I wouldn't mind watching Aries train. Does he ever take off his shirt? I laugh at myself and stretch. His bed is so large we could roll all over the place and…

I sit up and realize there's a dress draped over the side of the bed. Aries made sure I had suitable attire. While his long shirt is comfortable enough, I'm not about to parade through the castle in it for everyone to see. Especially not his mother. As sweet as she is, I can tell she cares a lot for propriety, and I don't want to risk making a bad impression.

Underneath the dress are some questionable undergarments

that I can't make heads or tails of. I get dressed as best as I can, not wanting to ask a maid for help like Aries suggested. I'm a big girl. I can dress myself. Besides, it feels weird to ask anyone for something so simple.

The last time I needed help dressing, I was probably four years old, and Hoc had been the only one around. For a moment, I'm lost in memories of him. My heart squeezes, and I blink back tears.

Shaking off the grief, I smooth out the lines in my green dress and check my hair. It's a bit of a mess, so I snag a ribbon from one of the undergarments and use it to tie my hair into a ponytail.

It'll have to do.

After a quick mental pep talk, I head to the door and open it.

There's no one around, and I hesitate, trying to remember which direction we entered from last night.

Before I can venture a guess, a young maid rushes up to me. "My Lady, do you need any help?" she asks anxiously.

"I'm fine, thank you," I assure her.

She eyes my dress but doesn't comment on it. "Breakfast then?"

My stomach is ready to rumble, so I nod. "Yes, actually. Food would be great."

"Do you wish to eat in here or…"

"The others I came with, do you know if they're awake?"

"I believe they are resting yet. I can take you to them if you wish."

"No. Let them sleep."

"If you don't have certain dishes in mind, I can take you to the tea room to eat."

"You already have food prepared?" I ask, impressed but also horrified. What if I hadn't been hungry? She would've gone to all that trouble for nothing.

"Of course," she says as if I'm the one being ridiculous. "The tea room is already laid out for you."

I smile warmly at her. "Well, please, lead the way."

She dips her head before guiding me down the long hall. After several turns that have me hopelessly lost, she opens a door and steps back to let me pass.

Inside is the tea room, which is apparently code for a dining room the size of my entire apartment back home.

The young maid follows me inside and then perches herself near the wall. On the table in the center of the space, the extensive spread of rolls, cheese, and fruit along with several drink choices is more than I could eat in a week.

Maybe we should wake the others after all.

I glance back at the maid.

"Is something wrong?" she asks.

"I can't possibly eat all of this by myself."

She frowns. "Should I wake the other guests?"

"No, no. They deserve to rest." I pause and then blurt, "You should join me."

Her eyes widen. "Oh, no, I couldn't possibly."

"Please? It's so wasteful to let it all just sit here untouched."

She bites her lip and then takes short, quick steps over to the table before perching on the edge of the seat farthest from mine.

"I'm Paige," I tell her.

"I know." She nods quickly, averting her gaze.

"And you are?"

She looks up, cheeks flushing. "Me? I'm just a maid."

"No one is just anything. What's your name?"

"Lucinda."

"Lucinda," I say. "Does anyone call you Lucy?"

Her eyes widen, and her mouth hangs open.

"Lucinda it is," I say hastily. "I'm not familiar with all the fruits you grow here. What's this?" I point to a fruit the color of raspberries but in the shape of tiny stars.

"That's a starberry."

I pop it into my mouth and immediately hum in pleasure. "It's delicious." I grab something else. "What about this one?"

"That one's called moon melon."

After she gives me a short lesson, which seems to make her feel better about sitting with me, I make sure that we both eat the fruit, and soon, Lucinda is relaxed and laughing.

"You really have a fruit called yucca?" she asks. "Is it gross?"

"No, it's actually pretty good."

She laughs again. "My sister would call that irony."

"So, you have a sister?" I ask.

Lucinda nods. "Brigita. She's older by two years. She's a scullery maid."

"What's a scullery again?"

The maid laughs. "It means she works in the kitchen," she explains.

"Did she help make these rolls?"

"Possibly."

"They're so good," I say.

"Aren't they?" She sighs. "Sometimes, we'll serve tiny cakes. She's given me a few to eat after feasts are over."

"You can have some whenever I'm around," I offer.

Her smile dims. "My Lady… That's not the way we do things around here."

I frown. "When I'm queen, I'll have some say, right?"

"Well, yes," she says in that wary tone that reveals she knows this is a trap.

"Simple then." I lean back and toss a stormberry into my mouth. Or try to. The blue-colored berry that tingles the mouth when you bite into it hits my chin and falls to the ground. I bend over and pick it up.

"I must admit, you are not what we expected…" Lucinda covers her mouth. "Forgive me—"

"Why? You can speak your mind," I assure her, straightening again. "I figured I'm not what anyone expected. Do you think others will mind?"

"Not once they get to know you. The people were so scared and worried when the prince was away, but he cares for you deeply, that's plain to see, and I think the people will grow to care for you too."

"Great. In that case, all we have to do now is stop an entire army of orcs."

Lucinda pales.

Wrong topic to bring up.

I ask her more about her sister and her family, and she opens right back up again. She seems perfectly happy with her role in life, and when I detect a slight change in tone when she mentions a stable boy, I can't help teasing her.

Eventually, Lucinda leaves to attend to other duties, but she gives me a bell that she tells me to ring in case I need anything.

"You know I won't ring it," I tell her.

"If you need anything—"

"Fine. I'll ring when I need a friend to talk to."

Lucinda looks like a deer in headlights. "My Lady—we cannot be—"

I wink. "We already are."

"Maybe," she whispers, and she hurries out of the room.

With a grin, I dip my spoon into a frost melon. According to Lucinda, the large pale-blue melons grow in icy caverns far to the north. The taste is a bit sweet with a cool, crisp aftertaste. It's refreshing enough that, for a moment, I let myself pretend this is my life.

Eating exotic fruit for breakfast in a kingdom I call home.

But the daydream doesn't last nearly long enough before reality edges its way in again. The truth is, this world isn't any safer than the one we left behind. If I'm going to survive in either one, I'll have to rely on more than just friendly maids and accidental alchemy.

6

ARIES

It wasn't easy leaving Paige in my bed half-naked and gorgeous while she slept, but being back in the training ring with Leo is satisfying—albeit in a much different way. We've been at it long enough that my muscles scream in protest, but I don't stop. I can't. Not when there's so much at stake.

I've already sent messages both to the council and to my generals. There's no time to waste, and if I'm going to restore us, I have to begin immediately. The training helps pass the time while I wait for a response. Not to mention letting off steam after yesterday's failure with Constantine—a vengeance I plan to take as soon as possible. Right after I slaughter the horde.

"You're going too hard," Leo complains.

He's not entirely wrong. I've been picturing orc faces instead of my brother's, and I've been fighting with everything I've got since the moment we began.

We've gained an audience by now. I wipe sweat from my brow as I survey the guards and soldiers who've gathered to watch.

"We'll handle the orcs," Leo assures me.

I grunt. "We haven't won yet," I counter.

He sighs, resigned. "Ready to go again?"

I grunt, and Leo attacks.

Sweat beads on my forehead as I counter his first swing. I take a step toward him, bring my axe up inside his guard, and angle the shaft so that the axe points at his neck.

"You would be dead," I say. "Again."

"You sound far too gleeful about that," he mutters, stepping back.

"We can switch over to lances if you like," I offer.

"You always best me with those things."

"I merely want you to become better so you don't die when the fighting is real," I tell him grimly.

"I…"

"You should have continued your training without me," I add, crossing over to the collection of weapons laid out on the table for us to choose from. I pick up a lance and hold it out to Leo as I place my axe down.

"How do you know I didn't?" Leo grumbles.

"Trust me. There's more rust on you than…" I trail off as I sense my mate. She's standing on a balcony on the second floor of the castle with Mag and Blossom. I wave to her, and she blows me a kiss before they head inside. I hope she's settling in well enough without me to help her, but I can't bring myself to call it quits for the day.

Part of me wants to fly out to the front lines. To offer assistance to the brave soldiers currently fighting in my name. Or better yet, demand the council even acknowledge that I've returned so I can re-take my rightful place as general of my army. So far, they've been completely silent.

Playing stupid fucking games.

But I can't afford to let my emotions rule me on either front. We need a plan. And for that, I need a clear head.

I select another lance and nod to Leo. We've just moved into position when Ferdinand, the royal secretary, approaches. He's been with us since Leo and I were kids, and his face is a welcome sight now.

"Ferdinand, good to see you," I tell him.

"And you, Sire." He clears his throat. "Forgive me, Your Highnesses," he says with a proper bow. "The Council summons Prince Aries immediately."

Immediately.

After not even bothering to acknowledge my return yesterday.

I nod to him and hand Leo my lance. "Thank you, I'll come at once."

"*We'll* come at once." I'm not surprised at all when Leo returns both lances to the table and falls into step beside me, Bingo at his side.

"You ready for this?" Leo asks as we walk.

I snort.

My parents used to bring Leo and me to meetings when we were kids. We were never allowed to talk or ask questions. We were just supposed to watch and listen and learn and keep our mouths shut. Since we were both never good at the latter, we were promptly removed and barred until we got older.

By the time we were teens, Leo had already veered away from any interest in the political side of princedom. I attended the meetings alone and then vented to my brother afterward.

Neither one of us wants to deal with these pompous men but according to my mother, they are the only thing standing in the way of full-scale counter-attacks against the enemy—and my ascension to the throne.

Ferdinand escorts us to the council meeting room, bows before opening the door, and calls out, "The princes have arrived."

I enter the room first, Leo right behind me. Ferdinand shuts the door behind us but not before Bingo slips through. Ferdinand looks scandalized, but Leo holds up a hand to halt him from retrieving the hellhound.

"It's okay. The beast is with us," Leo tells him and shuts the door with a click.

The council members have already claimed their seats, but they stand as I walk around the massive table to where my father once sat at its head. The king's chair is much more ornamental than the others with its high back carved with the image of a soaring dragon breathing fire.

Rather than sit in the empty seat, I stand behind it, my message just as clear. "Thank you for seeing me," I say, forcing the polite greeting.

On my right, Bran Beaumont, a bear shifter, meets my gaze. He's always had a rugged appearance and a muscular build. Today, he looks fiercer and more imposing than I remember. "Your Highness, we want to officially welcome you home." He frowns and then adds, "And we would like to know where exactly you've been."

On his other side, Thorne Davenport nods. The aging fae's dark hair remains unkempt, and the jagged scar running down his rounded cheek is not from the war but from an accident decades ago that he never speaks of. Rumor has it he tried to steal another man's wife, but it's never been confirmed.

"Is that right?" I ask.

Several of the men murmur in sharp agreement.

"As a matter of fact," Thorne says, "I believe this council deserves to know why you left in the first place, abandoning your kingdom when it needed you most."

More murmurs.

My temper rises swift and indignant. "It appears I am not going to receive a warm welcome from my own advisors."

"Welcome you?" echoes Porthew, a gray-haired man at the far end who served as one of my father's personal advisers before heading up the council after his death. "We are at war because of your desertion!"

"Watch how you speak to your king," I warn.

"You aren't our king yet," Thorne says darkly.

The fact that he dares utter such disrespect speaks volumes about the power they think they wield.

Leo clears his throat, and I glance at him. He shakes his head almost imperceptibly, clearly warning me to keep my cool. It takes all my self-control to do so.

"I did not leave of my own free will," I say, my words clipped.

"Are you saying you were kidnapped?" Porthew asks, his tone somewhere between mocking and mystified.

"No," I say on a sigh that does little to curb my impatience. "Magic, foreign to this land and more powerful than anything I'd encountered before, drew me to another world where I met my true mate."

Their expressions don't ease at the mention of my mate, though. If anything, they look more closed off. In this moment, I'm glad I didn't bring Paige to this meeting. It would only hurt her.

"Ah. So, you admit that you took a mate from another world?" Bran presses.

My eyes narrow as my patience slips. "That is what I just said. And why should it matter where she's from if the goddess has chosen her for me?" I don't give them a chance to respond before adding, "I would have thought you'd be relieved to see my duty fulfilled. I can ascend the throne. Strengthen our kingdom. End this wretched war."

"Not so fast," Porthew says. "We've discussed all possible scenarios."

"There is only one scenario—"

"And we've voted," Porthew finishes smoothly.

I glance at Leo beside me, but my brother is staring straight ahead. He's stiffened, and Bingo looks ready to charge. I follow my brother's gaze to see a robed figure lingering near the far wall. A maid? Since when are servants allowed inside during official meetings?

"Whatever you've voted on, doing so without the ruling monarch among you is a violation of your power." I look out over the gathering. "Look, war is an emotional business," I say, trying another tack. "But there are protocols in place. Laws. Tradition. I'm here now, so let's figure out how to move forward. Together."

Galen Chamberlain wearily rubs his forehead. His hair has been thinning for years, but what strands remain are as white as the snowy owl he can shift into. "Unfortunately, I'm not sure that's possible."

"And why is that?" I nearly growl.

"You aren't recognized as the heir anymore."

"I beg your pardon," I growl out. "I am to be king—"

"You abandoned Astronia." The robed figure steps forward into the light from a window. Slender hands reach up to push the hood back, revealing a familiar face.

Esma.

"Why he left doesn't matter," she continues. "Leo was loyal. Leo is strong, and he's proven himself capable. Our wedding never should have been called off for this… pretender."

"You have got to be fucking kidding me," Leo says, taking the words right out of my mouth.

Bingo lets out a low growl.

"You have no business here," I tell her.

"I was offered the position my father vacated when he died two months ago," she tells me.

I glance at Leo. "Is this true?"

He nods tightly, somehow looking both remorseful and angry at the same time. I want to ask why he didn't mention this before, but it will have to wait until we're alone.

"And where is the queen then?" I demand. "The council cannot meet or vote without the ruling monarch present."

"The queen vacated her seat." Porthew's glee is unmistakable, and it takes all my self-control not to punch it off his face.

"Why in the hell would she do that?"

Leo clears his throat. "Protocol," he says bleakly. "She did so yesterday morning before… If you hadn't returned, I would be king by now—and have her seat. But only if she vacated it first."

Fuck.

I'd interrupted too late after all.

"Do you want this?" I ask Leo.

"What?" He looks startled.

"Do you want to be king?"

"With her?" He jerks a thumb at Esma, clearly not caring if she hears him. "Absolutely not." He shudders.

"Just checking," I mutter.

I turn to face Esma, my blood running hot as my dragon's fury swells. "What you suggest—removing me as heir and propping up your own ruler—is blasphemy to the crown and to my father's law. Council positions are for serving the people at the pleasure of the king and queen. Nothing about you gives me any pleasure."

Esma squeaks, clearly insulted.

"In the absence of a mated king and queen on our throne, the council has had to take on the responsibilities and step up for the people of Astronia," Thorne says with an unmistakable note of haughtiness in his words. "We have made up for your shortcomings and thus have adopted new laws that allow us to govern while you, quite frankly, run off to who knows where."

I snarl, leaning across Bran far enough that Thorne flinches as I say, "You may have voted me out, but I will rip your tongue out for disrespcct if you speak to me like that again."

"May I see the list of governing laws you've adopted?" Leo asks sweetly.

Silence follows.

"Well?" I demand, my voice booming. "Where is this so-called list of laws that have given you the power to remove me as heir?"

"Here." Corian, one of the younger members, hops up and pushes a scroll into Leo's hands. Then he rushes back to his seat next to Porthew. The old man looks livid, but he doesn't say a word as Leo opens the scroll.

"Interesting," Leo says, scanning the document.

"What now?"

"You have indeed managed to pass a law that gives you the power to revoke an heir for abandonment." I start to interrupt, but Leo stops me. "You did, however, fail to remove the law that states anyone of the royal bloodline may challenge you all to a fight in order to win your seat."

"Excuse me?" Thorne asks.

Porthew spews a string of words that end in him coughing.

Esma puts her hands on her hips. "You're lying."

"Law number four-eighty-one," Leo says, tossing the scroll onto the table. "It's very small print. And very old. My father wrote it into the original council agreement as a measure of protection against corruption. It cannot be voted on or changed without dissolving the council entirely."

"You can't possibly remember a law that obscure," Thorne says, eyes narrowed.

Leo shrugs. "Check if you don't believe me."

Thorne looks at Corian pointedly, who jumps up and hurries to the table behind me where the law books are kept. Drawers are opened and closed before a thud sounds as he pulls out the book and scans for proof. A moment later, Corian makes a sound of protest and then whirls.

"He's right," Corian says quietly.

Thorne glares at Leo again, who merely says, "My father was

probably worried about people like you taking advantage. Anyway, a law is a law."

I fight the urge to smile as Esma scowls—and falls silent, for once.

The others have gone quiet too. I catch Thorne's eye, and he quickly looks away. Clearly, none of them like the idea of being challenged to a fight with me.

It's the first smart thought they've had all day.

Myantha Irvine lifts her hand. "If I may…" The female snow leopard waits for my nod of approval—it's the first sign of deference any of them has shown. "A compromise for the heir to earn back our vote of confidence."

"I'm listening," Bran says grudgingly.

"Let him lead the Astronian army against the orcs," Myantha says. "Fight and win this war for us. On his skill and strategy alone. Prove that he's worthy to lead our people. When we've won, he can have his wedding and his crown."

The council members exchange dubious glances as they consider it.

"I don't know," Thorne says. "Our vote is our word. If we go back on it, what message does that send to the people?"

"I could always challenge you to a fight for your seat," I threaten. "How about this afternoon? I'm free if you are."

Thorne's eyes widen. "I, uh…" He looks to Bran for help but gets none.

"Porthew," I call. "How about you? Willing to fight me to the death for your seat?"

The old man scowls. "Let him earn it," he says at last.

Myantha looks back at me, satisfaction lining her cat-like gaze. "It's settled then. Your Highness, the Astronian army is yours to command."

Esma huffs, but Myantha's words are apparently final as the rest of the group begins to rise.

The meeting is over.

I've been offered a single shot at regaining my throne from assholes who shouldn't have had the power to take it from me in the first place. I'm still debating on the fight instead when Esma marches up to me.

"This isn't over," she hisses.

Bingo snarls at her and lunges, but Leo holds him back. Barely.

"She's not worth it," Leo murmurs, petting the hound while staring the flamingo shifter down.

With one final glare at us, Esma whirls and stomps out. Bingo continues to curl back his upper lip until the door shuts behind her.

I look down at the hellhound. "I know exactly how you feel."

7

PAIGE

After breakfast, I go in search of the others. I don't get far before I spot Kitty chasing Zed down the hall. The gnome is screaming taunts and insults as he runs, a mischievous grin plastered on his face. Kitty is making a mewling sound that borders on feral. "Hey! You can't do that here," I hiss at them, grabbing Zed by his collar until his feet come off the floor, kicking wildly. "Now, take me to Blossom before I feed you both to a barn cat."

"We were just having fun," Zed complains.

Kitty huffs and tosses him a triumphant look that I can only assume means she's happy he's the one in trouble and not her.

I pin the raccoon with a glare so she knows she's not off the hook either. "I know you have manners," I tell her pointedly. "Use them."

She simply turns and lifts her tail, giving me a clear view of her behind as she leads the way.

When I arrive at their room, Blossom and Mag are already up and dressed. I can't help eyeing Blossom's pants and tunic with open jealousy.

"You look great," I tell her. "Where did you get those clothes?"

She shrugs. "They brought two sets for Mag, so I stole one." She gives me a once-over. "Nice dress. Isn't it supposed to have more layers or something?"

"Ugh, the undergarments freaked me out, so I skipped them."

She grins. "Is that the same as not wearing any underwear here? I wonder if Aries finds that sexy?"

"Shut up."

A maid brings them food on trays, the fruits and cheeses the same as the ones I had with Lucinda. I sit with them as they eat. No one brings up the Athenaeum. I wonder if, like me, they're just not ready to voice the facts aloud yet. We failed. Constantine won. And I have no idea how to stop him.

"I could get used to the food here," Mag says.

"It is delicious," Blossom says. "At least, this place has that going for it."

Something about her tone suggests there are far more things she doesn't like about Astronia than those she does. Before I can ask what those things might be, she sits back, rubbing her belly appreciatively.

"I can't remember the last time I had a meal I sat down for," she jokes.

"Sweetheart, I'll be your meal anytime," Mag tells her. "Especially dessert."

I groan and roll my eyes.

"I question why I'm with you multiple times a day," Blossom deadpans.

"You know you love it." Mag grins.

"There's such a fine line between love and murder," Blossom quips.

I shake my head. "You two fight like an old married couple."

Blossom pales, and I wince realizing the word "married" might have been a bit much for her—even as a joke.

"Twenty-seven is not old," Mag protests, slicing through the tension until there's none left. He looks at me. "Aren't I only two years older than you?"

"Only two?" I ask sweetly. "Feels like twenty."

Blossom snorts. "That's what happens when you age four times slower than anyone else," she says.

Mag and Blossom both come from worlds where time works a bit differently. The gargoyle might only look twenty-seven by this world's standards, but the real question is how long he's been that way. Blossom's done a better job at keeping her age a secret than him, though.

Mag eyes her, but he clearly values his life enough to know better than to ask how old she is. She doesn't offer it up, either.

"So, is your royal boy toy busy somewhere, being the big, bad dragon king?" Blossom asks me.

"He went off to train with Leo. He said he would be back soon, but I figured I would see how you all are settling in."

"You didn't want to be alone," she says knowingly.

"Nah, she just missed looking at a handsome mug all day," Mag jokes.

"All she had to do was call any of us," Ned cuts in.

"Definitely." I wink at the gnome.

I'm so glad that we're on better terms. We hit a rough patch for a while after I took over as Head Librarian. But even after all the bumps in the road, we're still family to one another.

"Well?" Blossom prompts after a beat of silence. "Are you going to finally tell us what happened to you when Constantine tossed you into that portal with Oliver?"

I nod, knowing it's time.

Mag and Blossom and even the gnomes are completely silent as I fill them in on what I saw. Watching Constantine consume my home world, including my birth family, and then watching myself remake it—all except for the people I wanted most to save. Then, I told them about seeing myself arrive at the library.

Hoc taking me in. Saving me. Protecting me. And finally, about Constantine's presence there all these years, biding his time, growing slowly stronger—and more determined to drain me forever.

"So, your magic is about recreating," Blossom says.

I nod.

"That's how you were able to make that portal for us," Mag says.

"It was a recreation of something that had been before," I tell them.

"That's amazing," Blossom says.

I flash a tight half-smile. "Yeah."

Mag's brows crinkle, and he opens his mouth, but Blossom cuts him off.

"So. The princes are training, hmm?" She points to the doors that open to a small balcony. "Maybe we can see from out there."

"Worth a shot," I say, relieved she's changing the subject.

Mag, to his benefit, lets it go too.

For now.

I follow Blossom onto the balcony and look down to see a large training area where a crowd is gathered. In the center is Aries. Leo too, but I have eyes only for my dragon.

As if he can sense me, and maybe he can, Aries looks up at me and waves. I can't help myself. I blow him a kiss.

"Really?" Mag arches a brow. "We're the disgusting ones?"

Blossom swats him. "What's wrong with that?"

"Nothing," he protests. "You're the one who made me promise no public displays."

The unicorn shifter ignores him and eyes me. "Do you want to watch them train or…"

"It seems like they're going to be at it for a little while yet, so maybe we can see about a tour?"

"I like that idea."

We head back into the suite. I don't like the idea of ringing the bell Lucinda gave me, but it's not like I have any idea which direction to go on my own. I open the door to their suite and ring it as loudly as I dare.

Lucinda appears less than a minute later. Crazy.

"What do you require, My Lady?" she asks.

"For you to call me Paige, for starters," I say.

She glances at the others, a little horrified-looking.

Or not.

"This is Blossom and Mag," I tell her. "And that's Ted—" I break off and glance around, but the gnomes and Kitty are gone. I sigh, hoping they'll stay out of trouble. "Anyway," I say, turning back, "We'd love a tour of this place if you have time."

"Of course, My Lady," Lucinda says, dipping her chin in hello to the others. "Where shall we start?"

I shoot Blossom a wry look before saying, "How about the library?"

About halfway through the tour, Blossom and Mag cut out, claiming they're going for a walk, but from the looks they're giving each other, I can't help but think they're walking straight back to their now-empty bedroom to be alone.

Lucinda finishes showing me the kitchens—only after I badger her into letting me see "behind the scenes" as she calls it —when another maid appears and calls her away.

"Are you sure you'll be all right?" she asks, hesitating.

"I'll be fine," I assure her. "I'll see you later."

She bites her lip but nods and hurries off. Alone, I wander deeper into the castle until I hear Ted's familiar laughter. My steps quicken.

I find the gnomes in a different tea room than the one I ate in this morning. I step in, surprised to see them sitting calmly. Then I realize they aren't alone. The queen sits at the small table in the center of the room, serving up what looks like some kind of vegetable.

"You'll enjoy this," she's saying as she passes them plates.

"It's green." Zed makes a face at the food.

"They're called sugarsnaps," she says. "Look." She picks one up and opens it. Inside aren't peas but a more cube-ish green food that glistens with, apparently, sugar. "They're delicious. Try it."

Zed looks skeptical, but Fred has always been a little more adventurous, and he tries one. His eyes open wide as he chews. "Not bad!"

The other three proceed to devour their own serving of sugarsnaps. I laugh as they scarf it all down enthusiastically.

"Oh, Paige! Come on in." The queen smiles warmly at me when she sees me lurking.

"Your Majesty." I make an awkward sort of bow before she waves it off.

"Please, call me Dorthea. And no bowing. You'll be a queen soon enough, and queens don't bow to anyone."

"Right," I say with way more confidence than I feel.

"How has your morning been so far?"

"I slept well," I say and immediately wince at the fact that I just referenced an image of me sleeping with her son. "And, ah, my maid gave us a tour. I hope that's all right."

"I should have given you one personally myself. Forgive me. I've been dealing with the fallout of the canceled wedding all morning."

"I understand. That must have entailed a lot of preparation."

"More than usual." Her expression sours. "I never did like that Esma," she grumbles. She covers her mouth. "Whoops. I shouldn't have said that."

I laugh and hold up my hand. "Don't worry about it. She seemed rather… persistent."

"More than you know." She sighs, and I get the sense there's more to the story.

"We're full," Ned announces.

Dorthea surveys their plates and smiles approvingly. "You did wonderfully. Tomorrow, we'll try a few other vegetables."

The gnomes exchange a wary look, but they don't argue. Apparently, the sugarsnaps were better than they expected.

"Can we explore?" Fred asks.

"Don't wander too far, okay?" Dorthea asks, although it's not really a question, more a command.

The gnomes hastily agree and bound out the door with Kitty hot on their heels.

Dorthea smiles after them then motions for me to join her at the table.

"You definitely have a way with them," I say as I take Fred's empty seat. "I could never get them to eat anything except junk food."

"It's nice to have someone to fuss over again," she says. A shadow passes over her expression, and she adds, "I worry at them being dragged into a war they didn't sign up for."

"We'll handle the orcs," I assure her, placing my hand on top of hers in a gesture that feels unfamiliar and yet comfortable. Dorthea is easy to be with.

She squeezes my hand. "I'm sorry if I drove Aries away."

I straighten. "Of course you didn't. Why would you think that?"

"After he disappeared, we all worried the orcs had somehow captured him. But when their armies began attacking us rather than using him as some kind of sacrifice for their coup, I realized they hadn't been involved. I worried…" She trails off, releasing my hand and dropping both of hers into her lap. She stares down at them as if embarrassed. Or scared. "I worried I'd been too overbearing with my insistence that he entertain all those women while searching for his mate. The law is archaic, but it exists for a reason. I hated to think I drove him away."

"You definitely did no such thing," I say firmly.

"I never lost hope that he was alive, you know. I could sense it. I'm not sure how, but I just knew."

"A mother's intuition," I say.

"Maybe. But it felt like more than that. The magic of my throne perhaps. What little is left of it. Either way, I'm glad he's home now. And that he's found you."

"Me too," I tell her.

I'm amazed that she sensed Aries through the portal. Outside magic shouldn't be able to pierce the library. Or that's what Hoc always said. Maybe Constantine's takeover changed more than I realized.

Worry gnaws at me over what other changes have happened in our absence.

"The kingdom needs you, Paige." Dorthea's words pull me out of my dark thoughts.

I frown, not sure I'm convinced she's right. "I get the impression not everyone will agree with you."

"You're different, and some people fear what they don't understand. But you have a good heart. Not to mention your powerful magic. A mage. The orcs will never expect that." She lowers her voice, adding, "Neither will the council."

I don't bother to tell her I'm not sure any of us should expect that. Or that even the word "council" triggers unease in me after what happened with Oliver and Tawny.

She stands, so I do the same, unsure of the protocol. Then she surprises me by embracing me. "Thank you for listening to a mother's worries. I have matters to attend to. Will you be all right?"

"I'll be fine," I assure her.

"See you for dinner, darling." She sweeps out of the room.

I linger when she's gone, eyeing some of the more exotic vegetables left on the table. Feeling adventurous, I pluck something that looks like asparagus but thinner—like cut grass. It's halfway to my mouth when the gnomes troop back in.

"Don't eat that!" Ned looks horrified.

"Why not? What's wrong?"

"It's a … vegetable." Ted shudders.

"You ate the sugarsnaps," I point out.

"The sugarsnaps tasted almost like candy. Almost," Fred says.

"The food is… Some of it is good," Zed says, forehead crinkling in thought.

"Some isn't," Ted adds.

"But we love it here," Zed finishes.

The gnomes all nod in unison.

"I'm glad," I tell them.

"And that's why…" Ned wrings his hands.

"What is it?" I ask.

He sighs and glances at Fred. Fred makes a face and nudges Zed. Zed stares me straight in the eye and drops a bomb. "We never want to go back to the library."

My heart skips a beat. Because, for a fleeting moment, neither do I. Is it so wrong to want my biggest problem to be an argument over eating their vegetables?

Unfortunately, I don't have the luxury.

"But we do want some candy," Ned quickly adds, and they all nod again.

I force a smile at them, letting their declaration pass for now. "Tell you what. I'll search the kitchens until I find you some candy," I promise. Every single one of their little faces lights up, and they cheer. "You guys don't get into trouble while I'm gone. Okay? Promise?"

"We promise," they chorus.

Famous last words.

I slip out and attempt to find my way back to the kitchen without help. The Athenaeum is huge, but it's nothing compared to this place—it's a literal castle after all—and I soon get hopelessly lost. Patting my pockets, I realize I've misplaced the bell Lucinda gave me. Probably left it behind in Blossom's room.

Giving up on finding the candy for now, I attempt to retrace my steps to an area that looks familiar. Finally, I recognize the guest hallway and wrack my brain for which one was theirs.

I knock on a few doors, but there's no answer until finally Mag opens a door. "Hey," he says.

"Hey." I exhale, both relieved and a bit defeated.

If I can't even navigate myself through the castle, how can I possibly hope to defeat Constantine? Or face off with an army of orcs?

"How are you holding up?" Mag asks, opening the door wider to invite me inside.

I walk over to a chair in his room and sit. He closes the door and crosses over to perch on the edge of his bed.

"Where's Blossom?"

"She went to check out their training facilities."

"You don't feel like fighting?" I joke.

"Figured I'd give her a head start to get warmed up. I was just about to come looking for you, actually."

"Me? Why?"

"To talk. To listen. Whatever you need. I wasn't just asking how you're holding up to be polite," Mag adds. His expression is serious, unlike the usual flirting and teasing he saves for Blossom, and full of concern. "And I'm not talking about the stuff with your magic. I can see you're still processing all of that, but ... There are a lot of expectations on you here. A lot of pressure."

"There were expectations when I was forced to be the head librarian," I point out. His concern reminds me of Hoc's protectiveness, and my heart squeezes with grief.

"Yes, but the library was your home. It was at least familiar. This kingdom is foreign to you, and you aren't just any couple here. You and Aries are *the* power couple. You're fated mates, and you'll be queen someday. Sooner rather than later, in fact."

"I've known for some time what I signed up for," I say, but his words prick at the same worries I've been trying to shove aside since we arrived.

"And you're okay with that?"

"Of course." I sigh, the truth spilling out of me. "Since I was a girl, I dreamed of leaving the library behind. Building a life here with Aries—it's all I've wanted since the moment I fell for him. But taking my vows to him, and more, becoming a queen to these people, means promising to put them first in everything. I can't do that until I deal with Constantine. If they ask me to take the throne before I've dealt with him… I won't be able to say yes."

"I get it," Mag says, and I look at him in surprise.

"You do?"

"Why are you so shocked?" he asks.

I shake my head. "I'm not sure Aries will be as understanding."

"First, I'm not Aries. Nor do I ever want to deal with the sheer amount of political bullshit that comes with being royalty." He shudders. "But I do understand needing to finish what you started. I think Aries would get that too."

"Thanks, Mag."

He straightens. "Now, stop sulking around."

I scowl. "I'm not sulking."

His brow lifts. "Since the moment we got here, you've been looking around like you're trapped and can't seem to find the exit."

"Shit," I mutter, covering my face with my hands. "Am I that obvious?"

"Relax, I have a feeling Aries has been too distracted to really notice. But you should talk to him. Soon."

"I will. I just don't want to add to his problems."

Mag rolls his eyes and crosses his arms. "No wonder you and Aries are mates. You two are exactly alike—always trying to deal with everything alone. Listen, when it comes to Constantine, *we'll* stop him. Not just you. As for this orc business, we'll help with that too. You do know that, right? We're in this together."

His words offer reassurance I didn't realize I needed. Of course, Mag and the others have my back. He's right. My stress must have been pretty high for me to have doubted that.

"Thanks, Mag. That means a lot," I tell him.

"Anytime. Besides," Mag adds, "With your kickass magic, that asshole doesn't stand a chance."

My confidence evaporates. I nod silently rather than admit how not-very-kickass my magic feels in the face of all these threats.

Mag rises. "I'm going to find Blossom and see if she wants to spar." He pauses, his gaze sharpening as he studies me. "You should come."

"I don't think I'd be much of an opponent for you," I say.

"Warriors come in all shapes and sizes."

His words spark something in me, and I push to my feet too. "Actually, I think I have more important skills to hone."

His brows lift. "Should I be worried?"

"Not at all. Well, not about me." I smirk. "Maybe about Blossom kicking your ass in front of the other soldiers training down there."

He winks. "Who says I won't let her win? There are benefits to needing your wounds tended."

I groan and shove him toward the door. "Go. Tell Blossom I'll come by to watch her victory when I'm done training for my own."

8

ARIES

"They're all insane." I stomp through the castle's halls with Leo on my heels. Between the council's outrageous vote and Esma's attempted coup, I'm not sure how much more I can take before I lose it.

"They're greedy men who see an opening for more," Leo grumbles. "If Father were here—"

"Well, he's not," I yell, whirling so quickly that Leo stumbles back.

He frowns at me, and my shoulders sag. "I apologize. I'm just so fucking pissed."

"No apologies necessary, brother. You have every right to be angry with me. I should never have let it get this far. In letting Mother handle it, I missed how bad things had gotten."

"No, it's not your fault." I sigh. "It's mine."

"It's neither." My mother's voice echoes from an open doorway just ahead.

I can't help feeling a bit of this anger aimed at her. She doesn't shy away from it, though, and instead waves us both into her office.

"Come. We should talk."

Inside, I stalk to the window, my dragon feeling more and more caged as the minutes tick by and reality sets in. Leo drops into a chair by the fire, leaning his head back. My mother surprises me by taking a bottle of whiskey from a desk drawer and pouring us each a drink.

"Here," she says, bringing me a half-full glass. "You need it."

"It's barely noon," I say, but I take it.

She offers a look of apology before walking over and giving Leo the other glass. Then she tips hers up, emptying it without waiting for us to join her.

Leo and I exchange a look.

I've never seen my mother drink outside of wine at official events.

He shrugs and then downs his own drink.

Fuck it. A moment later, I do the same.

When we're finished, my mother collects the empty glasses and returns to her desk where she remains standing. "I take it you've just come from the council meeting."

I force my voice to remain even, though I can't help the sharpness in my words when I answer her. "You should have told me."

She sighs. "I had hoped they would change their minds when they saw you in person."

"Well, they didn't," I snap. "I had to threaten them with bodily harm just to have the chance to earn my throne back."

Her eyes widen. She looks from me to Leo.

He sits forward and quickly tells her everything that happened at the meeting. I remain at the window, staring out while his words slice through me all over again.

"By the goddess, Aries. I am sorry," my mother says when he's done.

I don't bother to turn around before answering, "We should be fighting a war, not each other."

"You're right," she says. "They are blinded by their desire for power. When this is over, you must dismiss them all. Appoint an entirely new membership—"

I turn to her. "You're forgetting that I have to win this war first. Without the benefit of the throne's magic."

"It's not ideal," Leo says. "But it can be done."

I glare at them both. "You know allowing me to ascend the throne as a mated dragon king would strengthen the goddess' magic. We could wipe out the orcs with little effort or risk to our soldiers." No one contradicts me. "They are endangering the lives of our people to preserve their own stolen power. It's disgraceful."

"We agree, Aries," Leo says pointedly. "We're on your side here. Mom didn't just hand them the keys to the kingdom willingly. They did the same thing to her that they're doing to you. But we won't let them."

I exhale as his words hit home. He's right. My mother isn't to blame. And we won't get anywhere arguing between us.

"I should have just challenged them all to a fight and been done with it," I say darkly.

"The people will learn the truth," my mother says. "And they will see your temperance. Your patience. They will know that you've won this war by your brains and your own two hands. And they will love you even more for it."

"Mom's right," Leo says. "Take your anger out on the orcs, and let the council's own actions destroy them in the end. It's the better move politically."

My brow lifts at that. "Since when do you care about politics?"

He shrugs. "Since it helps you win the throne and gives me back my life as a second-born prince."

I shake my head. He's right, though. It is a better move. Just not as satisfying for my dragon at the current moment.

"Fine," I say at last. "But the people will know what the council's done."

"Absolutely," Leo agrees.

"And Paige," I add. "She needs to be kept as far from the council as possible until this is over. I don't want her exposed to their petty judgment and rejection of her."

"Consider it done," Leo says.

"Paige should be introduced to the people," my mother says. "They need to know her, to see how deeply she cares. Once they do, they will love and accept her when the time comes. It won't matter what the council says."

I nod, my thoughts and plans beginning to form as I consider various strategies for this war. It'll need to be a blend between combat and publicity, which only makes it that much more difficult. But Leo's right. It can be done.

And then I'll have my throne back, giving me the authority to toss the council out on their pompous asses—starting with Esma.

"I know that look," Leo says. "You're already strategizing."

"I am considering a few ideas," I say slowly.

He stands. "Where do we start? Tell me what I can do."

I blink, glancing around the confining walls. "I need to fly," I say.

"So, let's fly," Leo says.

"Are you sure that's wise?" my mother asks nervously. "What if you're spotted by the horde?"

I cross to where she stands and press a quick kiss to her forehead so she knows I'm not angry with her anymore. "Father trained us well," I say as gently as I can. "We'll be careful. But this is something I need to do if I'm going to lead the army."

She nods. "You're right. And Aries? I'm sorry."

"Don't apologize," I tell her firmly. "You're not the one who failed this kingdom. The ones who did fail it will pay."

She nods, and Leo and I head out.

"Well," Leo says, clapping me on the back, "This has been a fucking day already, am I right?"

I grunt as we walk through the castle, heading for the

northern exit. It's the best area for a swift and easy takeoff, but more than that, it's the location of the royal dragon stables. A building I didn't use much whenever I'd fly out on my own, but since Leo is with me—and especially after the council pointed out everything I've done wrong in their eyes—I decide to err on the side of protocol.

"It's not over yet either," I grumble.

"You'll feel better after you fly," Leo says firmly.

"Not as good as I'd feel ripping the council members limbs off their bodies."

He shoots me a warning look. "You promised to behave."

I grin darkly. "Relax. I'll keep my promise. Although, I do wonder how you knew about that law?"

"Just because I have no interest in the game of politics doesn't mean I don't know how to play."

I chuckle. "You're full of surprises."

"It's part of my charm."

He winks, drawing a laugh from me as we reach our destination.

The royal dragon stables have stood here nearly as long as the castle itself—with updates from each generation. Outside, it resembles the horse stables, but inside, the stalls are large enough to accommodate six dragons at once. There is no roof, allowing for beasts of varying heights and sizes access on foot or from the sky. Five generations ago, the stables were expanded after the king had four sons and a daughter—giving Astronia a total of six dragon shifters during the king's rule.

Our people still consider that century to be the most abundant and peaceful in the history of our world. I wonder if Paige has thought about how many children we might have one day. Unfortunately, that's not a conversation to have now. Not when the threat of two enemies hangs over our heads. But someday…

I enter the first stall, and my dragon tries to burst free before I've taken off my shirt. Impatient, I step out of my pants as scales cover my arms. In another blink, my hands and feet are replaced by claws, and my wings unfurl with a powerful whoosh.

Impatience wins out. I take to the sky before Leo has finished his own transformation.

What happened to you being the fast one? I telepathically tease him as he chases after me into the clouds.

Quick to start, quick to finish, he mockingly replies.

I laugh, my scaled belly shaking as I soar upward, relishing the freedom I feel to finally be up here. I stretch out my wings and do a few flips, twists, and circles to loosen up my stiff joints. My flights back in Paige's world were few and far between and always with the clock ticking on how long I dared to leave her alone.

Here, even with the horde's violence, I know Paige is safe enough down below right now.

Damn, this feels good.

My dragon lets out a roar just for the sake of it.

You want the horde to know we're coming? Leo admonishes, rising above the clouds.

They can't possibly have gathered this close to the castle, I scoff.

I hate to be the bearer of bad news...

At that, I stop arguing and join him higher up, my massive wings skimming the fluffy bits of condensation that obscure us from view down below.

Soon, the clouds disappear, and we're forced to go even higher to avoid being spotted. The air is thinner here. Colder too. But I don't mind it. Not if it means being airborne a little longer.

We've nearly reached the snowy mountains when I see them. A camp—larger than I've ever seen in this valley—packed full of orc soldiers. I increase my speed, needing a closer look.

You might want to hang back, Leo warns.

Why?

There's a reason the orcs have managed to destroy so many villages along our borders.

What reason is that?

They have developed a new technology of siege weapons.

What are you talking about?

Look. Down there.

He nods to the left of the camp, and I finally spot what he's talking about. Long-barreled and narrow, the gleaming black machinery isn't something I've ever seen in this world.

But I've seen it in another.

On Paige's television.

Depicting the most lethal violence I've ever witnessed.

My gut twists with recognition—and horror.

Bullets. Guns.

Manmade weapons capable of vast destruction.

Where did they come from? I ask.

No idea. Some speculate it's a technology from the fae in the outlands.

These are not fae-made, I say grimly.

Either way, our best guess is that the technology was stolen from somewhere.

Stolen.

Or given freely.

The council needs to know about this.

They do.

I grind my teeth together.

Don't shoot the messenger. Leo's attempt to lighten the mood doesn't get very far.

I have no idea how it's possible, but I do know guns like these could only have come from another world entirely. Brought through a portal. To be used against me.

Constantine orchestrated this. Even without proof, I know it's true. Just like I know all the way down to my bones that I'll defeat the orcs, whatever it takes, and then I'll return to the library and kill Constantine myself.

9

ARIES

When we return to the castle, Leo heads off to round up our top strategists while I go in search of Paige. Part of me wants to keep all that's happened today to myself, to spare her more stress. But I've seen what keeping secrets does to us, and I won't allow it to drive any more wedges between us again.

Besides, I need to feel her arms around me if only to quench the bloodthirsty beast shuddering inside my bones. Between the orcs' mysterious firepower and the council's political maneuvering, it's more than just my dragon that wants vengeance. It's the very essence of my soul. And since Paige is the other half of that soul, I can only hope she'll calm me.

But she's not in our bedroom, nor is she anywhere to be found in the castle itself. None of the guards have seen her. Even the maid looks mystified. My worry spikes as I imagine all the possibilities: the orcs stealing her away, Constantine finding us already, Esma—

Finally, I spot her strolling the royal gardens.

Hurrying around the hedges, I call to her. "Paige!"

"Aries?" She quickens her step toward me. "What's wrong?"

I catch her in my arms, holding tight as if the feel of her against me will chase away the fear. "Are you all right?" I ask, drawing back to study her.

"I'm fine." She looks wary now. "Are you? Did something happen?"

"Several somethings, I'm afraid."

"Okay, you're scaring me."

"Let's sit." With a grimace, I lead her over to a bench. Behind it is a hedge of rose bushes. Their white blooms seem out of place in a day filled with so much conflict.

"First, you should know that I'm going to do everything I can to fix it," I begin.

"Fix what?"

Quickly, I tell her about the council's stunt and subsequent deal for giving me back the throne.

"Wait, they took a vote to remove you as heir?" she asks, shock written all over her features. "As king?" she adds, her voice rising.

"Apparently, yes."

"They can't do that," she declares, shock turning to outrage as her cheeks flush. She blinks, adding, "Can they?"

"Unfortunately, they can and did." I tell her about Esma's involvement and Leo's knowledge of the law, including the one that says I can challenge them all to a fight.

She eyes me knowingly. "Please tell me you didn't do that."

"No." I sigh. "Leo and my mother both pointed out how that wouldn't be wise to win the people over in the end."

"They're right," she says, taking my hand.

"That may be, but unfortunately, this also means there won't be a wedding anytime soon."

A shadow passes over her expression. Something unreadable though I swear it looks almost like … relief.

"I see." She frowns, her forehead crinkling in worry, and then I wonder if I imagined such a strange response. "How do they expect to defeat the orcs without the magic from a mated dragon king on the throne?"

"That's part of the deal. I have to defeat the orcs without it. Then I will be recognized as heir, and we can be married—and crowned."

She exhales, and the way her shoulders sag, I can't tell if it's worry or the release of one. "Is everything all right?"

"Honestly…" She bites her lip.

"Paige, you can tell me anything."

"That's what Mag said."

My brow lifts. "You're taking relationship advice from Mag now? Should I be worried?"

She laughs. "No, he said you'd understand."

"Understand what?"

She lifts her gaze to mine, uncertainty darkening her lovely eyes. "I think… I prefer to wait to be married."

"Oh." I can't escape the jab in my gut her words give.

She rushes on to explain. "It's not about you. I want to marry you, Aries." She takes my hand as if to emphasize her point. "I have no doubts about you and me. It's just… once I'm queen, I'll owe these people my complete attention—and protection. I can't give them that just yet. I can't promise to protect this place as my home. Not with Constantine still wreaking havoc on what my home used to be."

"Mag was right," I say. "I do understand. And I think that sort of sentiment is exactly what will make you a great queen."

"Thank you," she says, her expression once again clear—and full of love. "And we will fix this. Council be damned."

I nod, needing to believe her.

"The orcs are no match for you with or without the goddess' magic," she adds.

At that, the sliver of relief fades, and I remember what news I came here to share. "I thought so too. Until Leo and I went scouting and I saw their weapons."

"Whoa, wait. What do you mean *saw*? You went to see them? Today? Without telling me?"

"Leo went with me," I assure her. "We stayed in the skies. No one saw us. It was a scouting mission only—to see what we're dealing with."

She exhales, still looking a little put out. "What did you find?"

"Leo calls them siege weapons, mostly because that is the only term that exists in our world. The technology—it's not something my people have ever seen. I have though. On television inside your apartment. In your world, I believe you call them guns."

"I don't understand. How would guns end up here in Astronia?"

"I can think of only one way," I say grimly.

Her eyes widen. "Are you saying what I think you're saying?"

"Constantine has been here."

"But… I have the book. It's in our bedroom—"

"I know. Either he's coming in another way or…" I take a deep breath. "Oliver told me he knew about this place, about the orc threat. He also knew I was a dragon shifter."

She looks stricken, and I can't blame her.

"Why didn't you tell me that? Before, I mean."

I shrug. "He was dead. I didn't think it mattered."

She nods slowly, her expression still troubled. "You think they planted these weapons? Armed your enemies before we even chose to return here?"

"It's the only thing that makes sense. These weapons didn't exist in this world before I left."

Her gaze drifts past me into the gardens. When she looks up again, fear reflects in her gaze. "We have to do something. We can't just let him win."

"We will," I assure her, squeezing her hand. "But the horde

has grown powerful, especially with weapons like these. We must stop them first."

"You're right. Yeah. Okay. Ugh, I guess this wasn't such a safe place for me to bring us after all."

I brush my hand across her cheek and am rewarded when some of her tension dissolves a little at my touch. "It was the perfect place to bring us."

She sighs. "I don't know about perfect. But I guess it was the right thing to do."

I study her, frowning as my thoughts return to the present moment. "Are you sure? You're out here in the gardens alone. If you're not happy here, I—"

"I just needed some fresh air," she assures me. "To clear my head."

"In that case, come with me."

"Where are you off to now?"

"I need to meet with my advisors. We don't have any defenses against these things. Your knowledge of how they work would be valuable."

She hesitates. "I'm not sure I'm qualified to advise soldiers."

I scoff. "And why not?"

She shakes her head. "I saw you this morning—sparring with Leo. There's no way I could wield a weapon like that, so I hardly think your men will take me seriously."

I smirk. "Is that what you noticed?" I ask, remembering the way she felt through our bond when our eyes met. When she blew me that kiss on the balcony. "I could have sworn you were too focused on the other thing I wield to notice how I fought."

"You did not just say that." Her cheeks flush, and I tip my head back, laughing at the effect my words have on her.

"Are you saying you weren't admiring—"

"Okay, okay. Busted," she cuts me off, and I grin.

"That's exactly why I want you beside me." I wink. "I fight better when I have you to impress."

Her mouth quirks at that, but she looks yet unconvinced. So, I drop the teasing and decide to give her the same honesty she gave me a moment ago. "The council sees you as an outsider," I admit. "They claim you aren't fit to lead our people since you aren't one of us."

"They're not exactly wrong."

"They're using it as an excuse to steal power," I say firmly. "It's a cheap shot. Don't let them land the blow."

She takes a steadying breath. I watch as that part of her that had begun to retreat into her shell emerges again. She squares her shoulders, and I can't help the pride I feel in her ability to find confidence in this moment.

"What should we do?" she asks.

"Let the people here get to know you. Show them who you are. How much you care. That you are willing to fight beside them. That you see them as more than a means to more power. Show them they matter to you and win their hearts."

"You think that will be enough to stop the council if they try to keep us apart?"

"Darling," I say quietly, letting my words scrape down the bond. She shivers, and I smile. "Nothing and no one could ever separate us again."

I lean in, crashing my mouth against hers in a kiss that's probably a lot more heated than it should be considering we're in broad daylight in the royal gardens. But Paige responds instantly, her kiss as feverish as mine. My cock hardens, and I seriously consider pulling her onto my lap and hiking this dress up to give us both some relief…

Fuck, this woman owns me.

But in the end, I ease back.

"Come," I say, my voice hoarse.

Her lips curve at the invitation in that single word. I grin, knowing full well what I just said.

"Come *with* me to the meeting," I add with a grin. "And when we're finished and I get you alone, you'll come *for* me."

She smiles wickedly as she leans in. "Is that a promise?"

AN HOUR LATER, PAIGE AND I ARE SITTING AROUND THE TABLE with my top strategists. Leo, Mag, and Blossom are among them. Bingo is sprawled by the door, napping, by the sounds of the soft snores. It's a strange mix of old and new, seeing so many familiar men among my new friends—and mate.

No one questions Paige's presence, but when I explain the technology and what it can do and then nod at her to take the floor, a few brows go up.

Then she starts speaking.

Her explanation of the weapons and their capability soon breaks through whatever skepticism they might have harbored. A couple of them begin peppering her with questions that she fields all on her own. By the time her explanations are finished, respect shines in their eyes.

She returns to her seat next to mine, and I reach for her hand, squeezing once lightly before releasing her. Through the bond, I send her my pride and approval.

She did well.

Unfortunately, that doesn't extend to the strategy of solutions.

"What kind of defenses can we mount against such things?" asks one of the captains.

"And where the hell did these things even come from?" asks another.

Paige and I share a look. Blossom and Mag tense. And Leo sees it all. I take a deep breath, knowing I can't put this off any longer.

"The world I went to housed many dangerous creatures," I say. "But the worst of them all is a wizard named Constantine. He is an evil man whose power comes from siphoning or draining the magic of others. When he tried and failed to drain Paige, I believe his anger led him to take revenge against me and my people."

"You think this Constantine supplied the orcs their weapons?" Leo asks.

"Yes," I tell him.

"But how would he have gotten them here in the first place?" Leo asks.

"A portal," Mag explains. "He uses them to travel between worlds."

"Is that how you got home?" Leo asks.

I nod. "Mag, Blossom, and Paige all had portal magic. On the day we arrived home, we fought Constantine and his creatures. He won and stole their portal magic. Paige was able to conjure one here so we could escape."

Leo's expression has hardened. It's obvious he's angry about the threat against us. "Can you portal back again?" he asks. "I'd like to have a shot at this asshole."

Mag, Blossom, and I all turn to Paige.

She frowns. "I'm not sure," she admits. "But even if I could, we need a plan. I won't walk us into battle without a strategy."

The other advisors murmur their agreement.

More respect.

"Does he have access to our lands?" Leo asks. "Can he come here anytime he wants?"

"No," I say firmly.

But Leo looks unconvinced. "Are you sure?"

"As sure as I can be. Why do you ask?"

"It's probably nothing... it's just…" Leo glances at all the faces assembled. His hesitation reminds me of last night's dinner. When I knew he and my mother were keeping something from me.

"If there's a threat, we need to know it," I say.

Leo sighs. "Mother—the queen has been keeping it at bay. But when we flew over the camp earlier, I saw that it had returned."

"What is it?" I ask a little sharper than I'd intended.

If Constantine has supplied some other weapon or threat—

"She calls it the blight," he says quietly. "The land… it's dying."

No one speaks, but the other advisors look just as shocked as I am.

"We assumed it was the goddess' magic receding. Without a dragon king on the throne… It started after you disappeared. The queen's fae powers connect her to the land, to nature. She used them as long as she could to heal the dead places. But… it keeps returning." His eyes are a bit haunted as he looks from me to Paige. "Do you think Constantine did this too?"

Paige turns to me, pale now. "He's draining this world. Taking its power for himself."

"How?" Blossom demands. "He can't get through."

"He can," Mag says grimly. "He must have figured out a way without the book."

Blossom's eyes narrow. She turns to me, a rage radiating from her that I recognize as a match to my own. "We need to find a strategy," she says flatly. "And soon."

No one else disagrees.

But when none are offered, the meeting is adjourned until we've all had time to brainstorm. The advisors are sworn to secrecy, and as Leo and I handpicked each one, I know they'll keep quiet.

The question is: Why didn't my mother tell me?

"I need to blow off some steam," Blossom says as she exits the meeting hall. Mag follows her, both of them headed for one of the empty training areas.

Paige and I fall into step across the courtyard. I slip my hand into hers and find it clammy and cold. She's shaken over the news about the blight.

"I—"

My words are cut short as a familiar voice rings out behind us.

"You need to stop holding back."

I stiffen, turning even though I already know who I'll find.

Esma stands at the edge of a sparring ring, snapping out criticism to the two soldiers in the center.

The others observing the exercise have moved as far away from her as they can get. But no one questions her presence. Not even the captain standing on the other side of the ring. It makes me wonder how many times she's visited the army's training grounds, sticking her nose in where it doesn't belong.

The fight ends, and Esma turns away, huffing as if the entire thing was a disappointment. I watch as she catches sight of us, a disgustedly haughty gleam lighting her eye.

She strolls toward us through the crowd of soldiers who part easily to let her pass. I start forward too, ready to tell her to get lost. But before I can say anything, Paige marches right up to the flamingo shifter.

"This is a closed training session. I don't believe you were invited."

"Excuse me, who are you again?"

Paige stiffens. The crowd falls silent as the soldiers tune into the exchange. Leo appears beside me, grabbing my arm before I can intervene between the women.

I stay quiet as Paige answers Esma in a loud, strong voice. "You know damn well who I am. And I know exactly who you are. A ladder climber who's only interested in one thing, and it's not these people's best interest."

"You know nothing about me," Esma says haughtily.

"I know you're not a soldier, nor have you been invited here by one."

"I'm a member of the royal council, which means I'm allowed to go anywhere I please. You're not even a citizen of this country. You can't tell me what to do."

Paige puts a hand on her hip. "I can, actually. As your future queen and Aries' mate, this is my house you're trespassing in."

"You think you can just waltz into Astronia and declare yourself one of us. But the people see you for what you are: an outsider. They will never accept you as their queen. You aren't even a shifter!" Esma screeches. She reaches for Paige, her hands up like she wants to claw out my mate's eyes.

I move to intervene, but Blossom appears, sliding smoothly in front of Paige, knocking Esma back a step.

"She might not be a shifter, but I am," Blossom says coolly, "and if you don't watch yourself, you're going to wind up with a horn up your ass."

Esma's jaw drops. "You can't speak to me like that."

"Don't act like you're innocent," Paige says, stepping around Blossom so they're shoulder to shoulder. "You've deliberately inserted yourself where you don't belong and not just here in this courtyard. You have no business as a member of the council when your only agenda is to grab a crown for yourself. From now on, keep your claws away from the princes. Neither of them is going to marry you, and that's final."

"You don't know anything about this realm or its laws. If something should happen to Aries, Leo will be king and—"

"Are you making a threat against the heir to the throne?" Paige asks, her tone low. "I might not be a queen, but I'm pretty sure you have laws about that."

To my surprise, two soldiers step out of the crowd and flank Paige. They stare pointedly at Esma as if they're only waiting for Paige's orders before dragging Esma off to the dungeons.

Esma's eyes widen as she takes in the soldiers. Instead of arguing, she starts toward Leo, her ire aimed fully at him now.

"You're going to let them speak to me this way?" she demands. "You're my fiancé."

"I am not," Leo says firmly. "We are no longer betrothed, and we never should have been. Paige is right. You orchestrated it all so that you could gain the crown for yourself."

Esma's eyes narrow at Leo as all pretense of caring for him vanishes from her expression. "You're going to regret this, you little—"

A growl sounds, and a sudden movement behind Esma draws my eye. Bingo rushes for Esma, teeth bared. I don't have time to warn her before Bingo's teeth sink into Esma's backside.

Esma screams, and Bingo immediately releases her, watching with satisfaction as Esma clutches her injured cheek.

She looks from Bingo to Paige then back to Leo.

"You should probably get that looked at," Leo tells her.

Esma's eyes widen as if she's finally realized she has no allies here. She ducks her head and runs away, shrieking curses at us all.

I watch her go in shocked silence. Eventually, I turn back to Bingo, debating whether to reprimand him, but then I note how Paige and the others are ducking their heads, hiding the same smirk I'm trying to keep off my own face.

Mag strolls up, a long sword propped over his shoulder. "What did I miss?"

10

PAIGE

Even after Esma is gone, adrenaline still courses through me. It's true, I'm not a shifter, nor am I a citizen of this country. What right do I have to stand up to her? Every time I'm tempted to second-guess my behavior, I remember how the soldiers backed me up. I can't be sure, but I have the distinct feeling that I could have ordered them to haul her to the dungeon, and they would have done it.

I'm not sure how I feel about having that kind of authority.

Or loyalty.

I'm not sure I've done enough to earn it.

But there's no time to dwell on it. Not after the news Leo dropped on us during that meeting. The blight changes things, reminds us all how urgent it is that we face what's coming. What's already here.

Aries announces the soldiers should gather around for their new assignments. I look around as the men begin to form lines—almost as if they all know exactly where to go… except me.

When I move to get out of the way, Blossom catches my arm. "Hey, aren't you staying for this?"

"I don't know. Are we invited?"

Her brow arches. "You're the future queen, remember? This is your house. You're invited everywhere."

She has a point, but I hesitate. "I don't know."

Aries walks up, slipping his arm around my waist and talking low in my ear. "Blossom is right. You should stay. Let them see you stand beside me."

There's a depth in his gaze that goes far beyond a moment with his army. My heart squeezes at the meaning. "How can I say no to that?"

"You can't," Blossom says lightly. "Where do you want us?" she adds, motioning to her and Mag.

Aries instructs, them and they move to take their positions. When they're gone, I look at Aries. "You're not mad?"

"About what?"

"The way I spoke to Esma..."

He snorts. "Are you kidding? I've never been more proud."

"Really?"

"Really." He leans in and whispers, "And turned on."

I shudder as he presses a quick kiss to my neck. The signal coming through the bond is enough to make me feel exposed, standing in front of all these people and thinking about Aries naked.

He laughs like he knows exactly what I'm thinking. Then he takes my hand and leads me to the center of the arena before turning us to face the crowd.

Aries' voice is clear and confident as he addresses his men. There's no hint of the worry I felt from him earlier when Leo told us about the blight. Or the guns the orcs have. "I stand before you, having returned from a foreign world where I battled a great threat on behalf of its people. I also found my mate in that world. A powerful, kind, capable female with the power to conjure and create worlds at her fingertips, and has brought us both home to Astronia where we will now fight alongside you to battle the threat to our survival here."

My cheeks heat as everyone turns to stare at me. But I keep my head held high for Aries' sake. Blossom catches my eye and winks. I exhale, relaxing a bit as I focus on my friends.

"The orcs think we are weaker without a mated pair on the throne, but they are wrong," Aries goes on.

"They're doing a pretty good fucking job for being so wrong," someone mutters.

Everyone tenses as they wait to see what Aries will do with the outburst. But Aries nods. "They used the element of surprise and our own disorganization against us. But no more!"

His voice booms the last three words, and the crowd quiets.

"You are Astronia's strongest, bravest, deadliest defenders. I have seen their numbers and their weapons. We will beat them, I have no doubt of that. But we must unite. To remember who and what we're defending. We are Astronians. We do not give up, and we do not accept defeat. This land has belonged to us since the goddess entrusted it to our care. We will not fail her. We will not fail our people. I am Aries Nemos, son of dragons!"

He raises his sword, and the crowd cheers.

The energy is a buzzing along my skin, a taste on the air, and I breathe it in, inspired by the faces looking back at us with so much trust and loyalty. It's kind of incredible standing up here like this. My blood pumps with the surge of their enthusiasm.

When they quiet again, Aries explains the guns he saw. Siege weapons, he calls them. The men's expressions turn grim—and deadly. He doesn't mention that he knows they came from my world. I'm glad for that. It's smarter that we focus on the orcs and the threat at hand without bringing Constantine into it.

Still, my mind wanders as Aries talks.

Between the orc's arsenal and the blight slowly draining the land, it's going to take a hell of a lot more than battle axes and blades to win this war.

It's going to take magic.

I can't deny the thought that whispers through my mind. Or

the fact that there's only one magic user standing in their midst. But I have no idea how to use what's in me against something like this. And I'm running out of time to learn.

Aries goes on to outline a grueling training schedule that will begin effective immediately. From now until we march for the front lines, everyone will be expected to train every spare moment. Despite the relentless expectation, I can't help but feel a little jealous that every warrior here already knows where they fit into the larger plan.

Even Mag and Blossom nod with matching expressions of anticipation like they can't wait to get started. I'm grateful they're here with us, but I also can't help worrying about how many of these faces will not make it home again when this is all over.

When the meeting ends, Aries squeezes my hand as the soldiers break off into groups. The ones in the fancier uniforms head for a small outbuilding nearby, Leo along with them. A few of the men in the group look back at Aries expectantly.

"How'd I do?" he asks me, ignoring them.

"You nailed it, Your Highness," I tease.

He smiles, his eyes sparking with an aliveness that wasn't there during our time in the library. "Thanks. I wasn't sure how they'd receive me back after the way the council rejected me."

"These men are not the council," I say. "It's pretty obvious they trust you and are willing to fight beside you."

He glances back at the men waiting on him. "I need to meet with the unit leaders. Do you want to come or…?"

He hesitates, clearly willing to let me join him if I want to. But I shake my head. "I'm going to see where else I can be of use."

"Okay." He brushes a thumb down my cheek. "I'll find you when I'm done."

I watch him walk off to join his men, who all shake his hand

and clap him on the back in warm greetings. It warms my heart to watch him with his people.

Finally, I turn back to look for the others and see Mag and Blossom standing among a group of soldiers. They're each being given swords and ushered toward the other fighters who are breaking into partners for sparring.

Turning away, I scan for other familiar faces. I haven't seen the gnomes in hours now and can only hope they're not getting into trouble wherever they are. Bingo is nowhere in sight.

On my own, I walk out of the training area and head for the path back to the gardens. The clang of weapons rings out behind me, and it only makes me more determined to work on my skills.

They have their weapons training; I have mine.

Except that I have no idea where to begin.

The only thing I know about my magic is that it can re-create what was once destroyed. How that can possibly help fight a war is beyond me.

I rub a hand down my face and kick a rock. It rolls until it bumps the trunk of a tree just off the path that is clearly dying a slow death—and looks to be just about there.

Hmm.

I walk up and stand before the ancient tree, its twisted branches hanging limp like the last breath was sucked out of it centuries ago. The bark is cracked and brittle, flaking off in patches. If my magic can do anything, I want to believe it can bring life back to something that's already lost its fight. If I can restore this tree, maybe I can heal the land too. Maybe even help in the war somehow.

I crouch down and press my fingers against the rough bark, feeling the dryness, the absence of life.

"I can do this," I whisper, trying to convince myself.

Closing my eyes, I concentrate, pushing my magic out, letting it feel its way through the dead wood, down to the roots, into every inch of what the tree used to be. I picture it alive again, its branches heavy with leaves, reaching high toward the sky. I can almost hear the rustling of wind through its restored leaves. I imagine it pulling water from the soil, thriving again.

But something cracks.

My eyes snap open just in time to see one of the larger branches splinter off and crash to the ground with a hollow thud.

"Ugh," I groan, stepping back.

The tree looks even worse now—if that's possible. Still lifeless, and now, missing a limb. Frustration burns in my chest. This isn't how it's supposed to go. Maybe I'm not ready for something this big. Maybe I'm rushing things—

"Focus," I mutter, forcing myself to try again. "You've got this."

This time, I reach deeper, calling on more of the magic inside me. I feel it pulsing through my veins, stronger now. I push it into the tree, demanding it respond. *Come on, come back to life*, I urge it. For a moment, I feel something shift, like the tree is starting to listen. I pour more magic into it, my heart racing as the wood begins to respond, the fibers realigning.

Then the ground starts to rumble.

Slowly, the tree begins to move—but not in the way I imagined. The bark ripples, almost like it's alive, then starts to crack. Thin, green tendrils sprout—not from the branches but from the roots. I stumble back as the dead trunk groans and bends unnaturally, like it's trying to free itself from the ground.

I take a step back.

Then another.

The roots, long dormant, now writhe like snakes, slithering across the garden floor. I watch, horrified, as the tree twists into something grotesque, its roots creeping outward, tangling through the dirt.

"Stop!" I throw my hands up, trying to pull back the magic, but it's too late. The transformation is already complete.

The tree—if you can even call it a tree anymore—stands

crooked and deformed. Its once-majestic trunk has become a gnarled mass of twisted wood, the roots sprawling out like some kind of creeping weed.

I stare, heart pounding.

This is not what I meant to do.

Swallowing hard, I step closer to the mess I've made. The tree isn't dead anymore, but it's not alive in any meaningful way either. It's something else. Something wrong. More like a shadow of life contorted into a shape that shouldn't exist.

I kneel, running my hand over one of the twisted roots. How can I use this against the orcs? How can I heal the land with magic that does... this?

I stand, brushing dirt from my hands, staring at the warped tree.

Turning away, frustration boils inside me. Maybe my magic isn't as useful as I thought. Or maybe it's just me. Either way, this mess won't help anyone.

"Hey," a voice says behind me so close that I let out a shriek as I whirl.

Aries offers a lopsided smile. "Sorry. I didn't mean to scare you."

I scowl. "It's fine. I was just… Never mind."

"Just practicing destroying our enemies?" he asks easily.

The easy way he phrases it has me scrunching my face. "Not quite. That tree isn't going to be battling in our name anytime soon."

"I wasn't talking about the tree."

"What are you…?"

His brow lifts as he nods at the wooden shards near my foot. "What did my childhood birdhouse ever do to you?"

Some of the wood is painted in bright blues and reds. Beyond that, it's no longer recognizable. Shit. I hadn't even noticed it among the mass of branches. "You built that thing?"

"Gave it to my mother for her birthday when I was ten."

"You're kidding. Oh crap, your mom is going to hate me."

He takes one look at my horrified expression and laughs. "Relax. She'll understand—and that's if she even notices it's gone."

He's probably right, but I'm not about to find out. I don't answer him, instead putting all my energy into sending my magic out to the pieces of wood lying in the grass at my feet. My magic is already coursing through me, on its way to recreate the birdhouse, when I say, "How about we don't give her that chance?"

"I have a better idea," he says, stepping closer. "Why don't we talk about what it would take to make birdhouses out of our enemies?"

11

ARIES

The next morning, I wake to find Paige snuggled in close beside me in our massive bed. The tunic I gave her to sleep in that first night has been replaced by a sheer gown one of her maids must have provided. The material is ivory in color and leaves little to the imagination. My cock hardens at the sight of her bared thigh draped over my own.

Back at the library, a wakeup like this one would have prompted me to use this moment to its full advantage. But now, my desire for her is at odds with the pressing need to fight.

According to my advisors in yesterday's meeting, the village has been re-opened, and the castle walls are now emptied of the townspeople who sought refuge here during the orc's attack.

What they had thought was a full-scale invasion ended up being only a single legion of orcs—most of them scouts who saw an opportunity and took it. Our soldiers weren't expecting the war to come here. Not when the majority of the horde's army was still camped in the north.

It's not a mistake we'll make again. Not with me in command.

Still, our scouts have returned with the news that the orcs are marching ever closer to our largest villages.

I can't remain safe behind these walls much longer. I might have left already if it weren't for the beautiful woman lying beside me. Paige will not be convinced to remain behind when I go. So, I've delayed as much as possible, hoping she'd discover her magic's true power at least enough to defend herself when we march to the front.

I cannot lose her.

And I cannot bear to separate myself from her either.

Yesterday, in the garden with that birdhouse, I saw a glimpse of what she can really do.

It was fucking amazing.

My thoughts wander back to her body, and I run my hand up her thigh, cupping her ass. She stirs, her leg lifting higher, and I stifle a groan as all thoughts of war slide away.

All that exists is my mate. Her body and mine.

My hand on her ass tightens.

"Mmm," she says lazily, her lashes fluttering.

"Morning, beautiful," I say, brushing her hair out of her eyes as she opens them and smiles at me.

I waste no time turning her onto her back and sliding down to position my face between her thighs.

"Oh, is that how we're starting the morning off?" she asks, sultry surprise giving way to anticipation.

"I'm starving," I say. "I was thinking I'd eat you for breakfast."

Her slow smile is sexy as hell.

I lower my head, ready to lose myself between her legs when there's a knock at the door.

Paige huffs out a breath.

I grin, ready to tell whoever it is to fuck off, but the knock comes again—louder this time. Paige yanks me back up, pulling the covers up too as she calls primly, "Yes?"

"Breakfast, Your Highness," the maid calls out from the other side.

Paige pulls the blankets up to her chin and calls out, "Come in."

"Good morning," the maid says as she enters and sets our breakfast on the table at the foot of the bed. She darts glances toward us without ever actually looking our way.

"Morning, Lucinda," Paige says.

The maid lifts her gaze and flashes Paige a tentative smile then ducks her head again as she heads for the door. "Will there be anything else?" the maid asks, hovering with her hand on the latch.

"No, thanks," Paige tells her.

"I have your dress for the day already laid out," the maid says. "I can bring it in as soon as you're finished eating."

"Thanks," Paige says.

The maid smiles again and then leaves us.

My brows lift at the friendly exchange. "Are you two best friends then?"

"Lucinda's been really welcoming," Paige says, tossing back the covers and kicking her legs over the side of the bed.

I grab her waist, pulling her back before she can fully escape. "Whoa, where do you think you're going?"

"You heard her," Paige says, not bothering to fight me as I pull her onto her back and into my arms. "She's returning soon, which means we're going to continue to be interrupted." She grins. "Unless you can start and finish in the next five minutes."

"Five minutes? You think I'll have had enough of you by then?"

She laughs, and for a moment, I lose myself in the sound of it. The sight of her smile after the last few days—or weeks—is a drug, and I'm determined to have more.

I kiss her loudly then grab her hand, hauling us both up. "Come on," I say.

"Where are we going?"

"Somewhere we won't be disturbed."

"This is where you change forms?" Paige asks an hour later as she gazes at a stall. "It's massive!"

"Dragons take up a lot of space," I say smugly.

She tosses me a smirk before turning back to the empty stalls.

"One, two… Six. There are six dragons in your family?"

"There were. A few generations back. But not since then."

"So many," she murmurs.

"Now, only two." I can't stop myself from wincing. "And if we don't win my crown back from the council, we may be the last."

She places a hand on my arm. "You will. We will," she corrects. "Together."

I wait for her to mention the library, but she doesn't, and I exhale. It's a problem that isn't going to fix itself, but I don't want to think about it today. "Are you ready?"

"Ready for what?"

I wink. "A ride."

I watch as the innuendo sinks in. Her cheeks flush, and she glances around, her voice hushed as she says, "This isn't any better than our bedroom. Not when anyone could walk in and see us."

"Which is why I was thinking I'd shift and you could fly with me for a bit."

"Oh!" She winces, and her cheeks are as red as tomatoes. "Ah, can you forget I just said all that?"

"Not a chance," I say smugly. "Besides, you're on the right track. That's still the end goal."

She groans and then looks around again, but we're

completely alone here—for the moment. I step into the stall before I can change my mind and hike her dress up against one of these walls. When I begin stripping out of my clothes, Paige's expression pinches.

"Um, is there a saddle? Or a harness or something?"

"Nope."

"How am I supposed to hang on?"

"I won't let you fall."

"And if I happen to, you'll catch me with your claws and not impale me." She gulps.

"If you're too scared to, I understand," I say in the same tone I would use with Leo when I want to goad him into doing a dare.

"I'm not a child," she protests, eyes narrowing. "And I'm not falling for that tone either."

"So you don't want to see the kingdom you're going to rule someday?"

"No, I want to." She bites her lip. "Will we only fly near the castle?"

"We will not go near the orcs," I assure her.

"What if I want us to?" she asks.

I shake my head, ready to argue if necessary. "You aren't ready to fight them yet."

"I'm not asking to fight. I just… I want to see their camp —and their weapons—for myself. If I'm going to damage them, I need to know how to prepare. How to hit them and where."

I remember what she did to the birdhouse and nod slowly. "All right. I'll take us as close as I can without being spotted."

"Thank you."

I bring her hand to my mouth and brush a kiss over her knuckles. "I'm not sure I could refuse you anything. Now, do you trust me to take you for a ride?"

She lifts her brows. "In which way?"

With a laugh, I gesture for her to step back into the hallway that runs down the middle of the stalls, and I finish stripping down.

Paige lets out a low whistle. “That sight never gets old.”

I growl, impatience driving me to shift quickly now.

Bones pop and creak as the change takes me over. Scales coat my skin. Followed by claw and tooth and a fire burning like a furnace in my very soul. Within moments, I am a winged beast ready for the skies.

“Um, you never told me how to climb up,” Paige squeaks up at me.

I extend my wing down, and she gapes at me.

“You want me to step on your wing? Won’t that hurt you?” she asks.

I snort, air gusting from my large nostrils. Silly woman. Her tiny form won’t hurt me.

She scrambles up and then sits high up on my neck. “Where do I… Oh.”

Paige’s hands grab for my scales, and I beat my wings against the stall air until I begin to rise into the sky above.

We leave behind the dragon-changing building, and Paige lets out a shriek as we head toward the castle. I’m careful not to dip right or left as I gain altitude, wanting her to enjoy this experience as much as I do. With the wind singing along my scales, I feel Paige relax. Her fear becomes pleasure through the bond, and it makes me braver.

Just ahead is the castle, and Paige urges me toward it.

I soar around turrets, and a banner brushes against my belly as we speed by. Her grip with her thighs and hands is tight at first, but once I slowly turn away from the castle toward our destination, she eventually loosens her hold—trusting me to keep her upright. To keep her safe.

I do a few dips and rises to give her a thrill, but finally, I level out and fly onward for the orc camp. The clouds provide cover that I gratefully use the closer we get to their camp. Just like before, with Leo, I'm careful to keep a safe distance from their scouts. And still, I'm tense as the camp comes into view far below.

The clouds offer a wispy film between us and the camp, but it's still visible enough far below us now. Tents and campfires litter the valley. And there, along the outskirts of the camp, their guns sit quietly. Beside them is a convoy of carts full of various ammunition.

Paige's grip on me tightens, and I know she's seen them too.

I do one full wide arc around the camp and then head away from it as fast as my wings will carry us. The moment we're in safer skies, I let out a relieved exhale. On my back, Paige remains tense, and I can sense her thoughts darkening as we fly. No doubt, she's thinking about those weapons we're up against–and what she might do to them with her magic.

I'm determined to take her mind off such worries even if only for a while.

When we reach the forest that signals the royal grounds, I turn away from the castle and head for a different destination farther north. The cliffs rise high on the far side of the trees—their sheer face a myriad of reds and oranges lit by the sun at our backs.

The sight of it sends a pang of familiarity through me after being gone so long. With a final swoop, I take us down, landing at the mouth of the cave I secretly call my own.

Paige slides down my offered wing and looks around as I return to my human form.

"Holy shit, that was amazing," she says. "The wind was incredible! And the view. Speaking of which, I must look like a mess. My hair…" She tries to pat it down, but I don't care about that. Doesn't she realize that she's perfect as she is? She doesn't have to change a thing. She has my entire heart.

"My love," I murmur. "You look perfect."

Her smile is slow but stretches wide and full. "My mate," she says, her hand coming up to rest on the side of my face. "Thank you for letting me fly with you."

In answer, I crush her lips with mine, my arm snaking around her waist as I yank her so close against me that there's hardly any space between us.

Just her infernal clothes.

"You look beautiful in this dress," I murmur.

"You like me in the clothes of your people?" she asks breathlessly.

"I like you in everything, but I prefer when you aren't wearing anything at all."

I press her against the cave wall until I know she can feel the erection that's almost painful now that we're finally alone.

"Here?" she asks.

"Why not?" I nuzzle her neck before trailing a line of kisses along her collarbone.

She breaks off the kiss. Worse, she takes a step back—but then she lifts her dress over her head and drops it beside her.

My hunger for her burns inside me.

"You're not wearing any undergarments," I manage.

She smirks. "I don't like how they constrict."

"We wouldn't want that," I say, reaching for her wrist and yanking until she's inside the circle of my arms again.

I kiss her deeply, plunging my tongue into her mouth, claiming her as if it's the first time all over again. My hands grip her hips, pulling our bodies flush as I back her against the cave wall. Breaking our kiss, I dip lower to her neck, her collarbone, her breasts, leading the way with my roaming hands. Her bared breasts fill my palms, their weight perfect, her skin smooth and velvety.

Taking her nipple into my mouth, I suck hard, enjoying the tiny gasp she lets out as well as the arch in her back.

Her hand finds my cock and wraps around it. I groan, all coherent thought flying out of my mind as she grips me. She uses a foot to move her dress in front of me and kneels on top of it. I suck in a sharp breath as she parts her lips, her gaze fixed on my face as she licks the tip of my cock.

"Paige…"

My hands fall to her head, and I grip her hair as she takes my cock into her mouth and sucks me.

"If you keep doing that…" I rasp.

"Mmm," she says around my cock, the vibration alone enough to make my cock jerk again.

"Come here," I growl after only a few moments.

I pull my cock out of her mouth and guide her to her feet. My lips touch hers briefly before I bend down and fumble with her dress, stretching it out so it can serve as a blanket.

I need her—now.

Paige melts against me as I lay her down on top of the soft material. My hands glide over her skin, drawing sounds of pleasure from her as I flick my thumb over her hardened nipples. Then lower to her wet heat where I push a finger inside her.

She tenses, her fingernails scraping over my shoulder as she rocks her hips to meet me. Slowly, I draw my hand back and lick her taste off my finger.

Paige's eyes track the movement. "Aries…"

"Fucking delicious." I wink. "Time to return the favor."

I bury my face between her legs, running my tongue over her clit before lapping up her sweet juices. Paige gasps, her hand grabbing my hair as she squirms beneath me.

Possessiveness rises inside me, my dragon reveling in the way this woman has given herself to me. In this moment, every inch of her belongs to me, including this sweet nectar.

Paige's legs start to tremble, and she cries out as she comes for me. I don't stop licking and sucking until her sounds stop and her breath exhales in a whoosh. Then I lift my head and cover her body with mine. I pause there, looking down at her uncertainly.

"Have you had enough?" I tease.

But she reaches for my hips and pulls me down, grabbing my cock and guiding it to her entrance.

"Never," she whispers.

I enter her with one thrust, and Paige gasps, her hands wrapping around my neck as our bodies begin to move together. Her core is a delicious heat, and I'm very nearly ready to lose myself to it. Our pace is slow at first, our mouths meeting in lazy, languid kisses. But the pleasure inside me–and through the bond–builds to a crescendo, and I move my hips faster, my thrusts harder and more urgent as we both give ourselves over to this moment.

Now, Paige is the one who owns me, her every move both demanding and coaxing more and more of what I willingly and hungrily offer. Her body trembles beneath me, her muscles tensing until she's coiled tight.

We both are.

Still, I don't stop, my pace relentless now. Sweat coats my skin and hers.

She clings to me, her nails raking down my back as she holds on, her hips moving in rhythm to match me.

Then she whimpers my name, and I feel her entire body go slack as she comes for me. It's all I need to send me over the edge along with her.

"Mine," I snarl as I empty myself deep inside her.

12

PAIGE

Aries sighs contentedly as he lifts his head to look down at me. The cave floor is cool beneath me, but I don't mind it after working up a sweat just now.

"Do you want to shower?" he asks, brushing my hair back from my face.

"Shower?" I blink in confusion.

His grin is slow and lazy. "We can get freshened up before I show you around the rest of this place."

"You have a shower here?" I ask, not sure whether to be impressed or leery. It is a cave, after all. How nice can the shower really be?

He chuckles. "I'm a dragon. Did you really think I would bring you to an ordinary cave?"

"In that case..." I kiss him quickly. "Can we shower together?"

He grins. "I think we can make that work. Come on."

Aries helps me up and grabs my hand. We're both still naked as he leads me through a narrow opening along the back wall. On the other side, I find myself in a beautiful passageway glittering with precious stones inlaid along the walls that gleam in the light filtering in through the cracks far above our heads.

"Wow," I breathe, admiring the way the passage is open all the way up to the ceiling of smooth stone. "It's so pretty."

"We're not even there yet," he says with a chuckle.

A moment later, the passageway ends, and we step through another opening. I falter, shocked into silence as I attempt to take it all in.

The cavern is large–much larger than the one we entered from. The temperature is cool but not cold and is well-lit thanks to the light filtering in from above. The far side of the space is piled high with gold coins, jewels, and items made from silver, including a giant candelabra that looks more expensive than my entire apartment back home.

I look at Aries questioningly.

He shrugs. "I'm a dragon; what did you expect?"

I shake my head, laughing as he tugs me to the left.

I turn away from the treasure glinting in the sunlight, and that's when I finally notice what he referred to so casually as a shower. Except it's not a shower at all; it's a waterfall that cascades into a serene pool. The walls on its three sides glow a slightly purplish hue that paints the entire place like a fae wonderland. I walk to the edge and peer down, noting the crystal-clear water that reveals a smooth bottom.

Still, I brace myself for a chill and am shocked when I dip my toe in and find it as warm as bathwater.

"How do you keep it so hot?" I ask, wading in behind Aries.

"This mountain stands atop a hot spring," he explains. "It's what regulates the cave's temperature and keeps the waters so warm."

"And the purple?"

"Amethyst stones."

Before I can ask anything else, he dunks himself under the water. With a happy sigh, I do the same. When he re-emerges, he swims to the far end and shows me a small alcove carved along the wall stocked with soaps.

I can only shake my head. He's right. Here I was, expecting a normal cave–not a mistake I'll make again with my resourceful dragon.

We take turns washing under the gentle waterfall, and I can feel the tension draining out of my muscles beneath its hot spray. For these few moments, the outside world doesn't exist for us. No orcs invading this land, no evil wizard attempting to destroy the worlds for his own gain. There's only Aries and me and this safe haven he's made for us.

It's soothing in ways I didn't know I needed.

Once we're all clean, I splash Aries, and we have a water fight that turns into lovemaking in the gentle waves. But soon after, reality begins to press in around the edges. We need to get back before we're missed. There's too much at stake to remain here forever.

Eventually, Aries helps me out of the pool and guides me over to another carved rock that has towels and even a robe waiting. Aries holds the robe out to me, allowing me to slip my arms inside before wrapping it around myself.

"I see you've thought of everything," I tease. "How many girls have you brought here exactly?"

"I've never brought anyone here," he says.

I stop wrapping my hair in a second towel and gape at him. "Not even Leo? Why not?"

He chuckles. "Dragons are territorial about their lairs. The only one my beast would ever allow to see this place is his mate."

I press a kiss to his mouth. "I'm honored. Does that mean your dragon anticipated your mate needing another dress?"

He grins. "What kind of treasure hunter would I be if I didn't have spoils for my woman?"

We head back through the glittering passageway, stopping at

one of the small openings we passed earlier. I laugh as I realize we're standing inside what is essentially a walk-in closet.

Aries motions to the dresses hanging on the right. "Take your pick."

I sort through the dresses, choosing a blue one that matches Aries' eye color. He helps me put it on and lace it up. I try not to worry about what Lucinda will think when I arrive in a different outfit than when I left.

When I'm ready, Aries takes my hand and leads me back to the mouth of the cave.

The view from here is gorgeous, and I can see how wonderful it will be here once the war is over, but then my bubble shatters. Off to the east, I spy a destroyed village, and my heart sinks. Even from afar, I can see the effects of a fire.

"The orcs…" I say.

Aries nods grimly. "They marched right through the village rather than taking the road around it."

"Wait, this just happened?"

"Yesterday."

I turn to him sharply. "You knew?"

"Our scouts brought word late last night. By then, it was too late for reinforcements." His hands are fisted, and I can feel the fury radiating through the bond.

"All day," I say, "you knew, and you didn't say anything."

It's not an accusation. But I can't help wishing he'd let me help shoulder some of the worry he's carrying.

"I wanted to have a few hours where it was just us," he admits quietly.

The weight of what we're up against hits me in a way it hasn't before now. It's more than the destroyed village or the loss of control of the Athenaeum. It's everything at once.

The lives lost.

The lives still depending on us for survival.

Aries' crown.

I blink back tears as guilt for it all presses down around me. "Aries, I'm so sorry. This is all my fault."

He makes a face and shakes his head. "The orcs did this."

"But if you had been here instead of with me—"

"If I hadn't come through the portal, I never would have found my fated mate," he points out.

"And Constantine would never have supplied your enemies with weapons of destruction."

Not to mention the blight draining Astronia of its magic.

"Hey." He grabs my chin in his hand. "We can't afford regret." He brushes his thumb over my cheek. "With my father gone so suddenly, the war would have happened eventually. And if I hadn't come to the library when I did, you would have faced Constantine alone. This is our destiny, Paige. The good and the bad. We'll face it together."

I weave my fingers through his. "Together," I echo, ignoring the hollow pit in my stomach as I think about how many others before me have already been lost to destiny.

Hoc.

My birth parents.

The entire library.

I can't help feeling like fate is nothing more than a tidal wave of loss intent on wiping out everything in its path. And I'm not sure there's anything we can do to stop it.

HOURS LATER, I SIT ON A STONE BENCH IN THE CASTLE GARDENS, tucked into a secluded corner I found, knees pulled to my chest, staring at the fading light filtering through the trees. The guilt from earlier twists in my gut, heavy and suffocating. The village... all those people. I should've found a way to send Aries back here sooner. Maybe then, they'd still be alive.

I hear footsteps behind me and tense. Aries already said he'd be gone the entire evening, doing training exercises. Blossom and Mag are undoubtedly doing the same, which leaves a very short list of people I want to summon a brave face for at the moment.

"I'll be right out," I say without turning around, hoping whoever it is will take the hint and leave.

"Yeah, I'm sure you will." The voice is familiar, though we haven't spoken much. I glance over and find Leo standing in the small opening between hedges, hands in his pockets, watching me carefully. "You looked like you could use some company."

I blink, surprised he's here. Leo and I haven't really had a one-on-one conversation—beyond him professing a life debt to me for saving him from marrying Esma. He's always with Aries, cracking jokes or offering support to his big brother—and me by extension. But now, there's a quiet scrutiny in his eyes as he focuses on me.

"I'm okay," I say, trying to wave him off. I'm not exactly in the mood for whatever banter he's famous for.

He shrugs then steps farther into the little alcove. "The problem is this is my favorite brooding spot too. So, I guess we'll just have to share."

I glance at him, half-expecting a cocky grin, but his expression is softer than I thought it'd be. Still, I try to brush him off. "I'm not brooding. I'm…processing."

"Ah. Is that what they call it in your world?"

I snort but can't quite summon a smile.

He doesn't seem to mind.

A moment passes, and he doesn't move to leave.

I try to ignore him, but the quiet presses in too hard. "It's the village," I finally say, my voice quiet. "All those people... it feels like I should've done something to stop it."

Leo stays silent for a moment, and I half expect him to crack another joke. But when he speaks, his tone is serious. "It's not your fault. You know that, right?"

I rub my hands together, trying to get rid of the nervous energy coursing through me. "Logically, I know that. But I also know there are more villages at stake. And what if... what if we lose? What if I can't do enough to help? Every time I try, I feel like I'm just... failing."

His expression softens. "I know how you feel."

I think of the way he's always smiling and laughing. At the way he wields a sword in the training ring with Aries. And I shake my head. "No offense, but I doubt that's true."

Leo straightens, crossing his arms over his chest. "You think I'm not scared of that exact thing?"

I glance over at him, surprised by the rawness in his voice. "Are you?"

He snorts. "I've been scared since the moment Aries left for your realm and, suddenly, everyone was looking at me like I was supposed to have the answers." He shakes his head. "I'm the second-born prince. I'm not supposed to be the one leading armies or making big decisions. That's Aries' job. I'm just the backup. The spare."

I frown. "You're more than that."

"Don't get me wrong. I have no desire to rule. But when it's thrust into your lap and you have no choice but to step up… it's terrifying." Leo chuckles, but there's no humor in it. "Feeling like you're not enough? That's a feeling I know very well."

He's quiet for a moment, and I feel the weight of his words sinking in. I never realized how much he carried with him. All this time, Leo's been acting like everything's fine, but underneath, he's been struggling too.

"I thought you were always so confident," I admit, almost embarrassed at the way I'd dismissed what must have been a difficult role for him.

"For a long time, my confidence was mostly smoke and mirrors. It's easier to pretend you're not scared when you've got a whole kingdom who sees you as the funny, carefree prince. But the truth is, every day Aries was gone, I woke up wondering if that was the day I finally screwed it all up. Lost the kingdom. Got people killed."

I blink, taken aback by his honesty. "Then... how do you keep going? If you feel like that all the time, how do you keep moving forward?"

Leo turns to me, his expression softening. "Because it's not about me. It's about them. The people we're fighting for. The ones who believe in us, even when we don't believe in ourselves."

I look down, his words hitting me hard. "But what if we fail? What if we lose everything?"

"We might." His voice is steady. "But that doesn't change the fact that we have to try. We keep pushing because people are counting on us. Not to be perfect but to be there. To show up. And, Paige, you've already done that. You've already shown more strength than most people ever could."

I shake my head. "I don't feel strong."

"You don't have to." Leo leans closer, his voice dropping to a quiet, serious tone. "Strength isn't about feeling strong. It's about what you do when you're scared out of your mind. You think I don't want to run in the opposite direction sometimes? You think Aries doesn't feel the pressure? We're all terrified. But we fight anyway."

I can feel the tightness in my chest loosening just a little. I glance over at Leo, his face open and honest. "You really think I've made a difference? I'm not even Astronian."

He gives me a half-smile. "Aries' utter devotion to you aside, I see the way the men look at you. Like they respect you. Like they'd fight for you. Hell, even my mother likes you. That's gotta mean something, right?"

For the first time all day, I feel something shift inside me. A spark of confidence. And more than that, hope.

"You know," I say, "for a guy who usually jokes around, you're not half bad at pep talks."

Leo grins. "Don't tell Aries. He'll never let me live it down."

I laugh softly, the sound surprising even me. "Thanks, Leo. I needed this."

He stands up, stretching his arms over his head. "Anytime. Just remember, Paige—courage isn't about being fearless. It's about pushing through the fear. It's about being willing to face something so the rest of our people won't have to."

"Wow, you should give a speech or something."

"Nah, I stole those words from Aries, who stole them from our father."

I laugh, shaking my head.

As he turns to walk away, he calls back over his shoulder, "I hope this means I get my favorite brooding spot back."

I watch him go, feeling the weight on my chest lift just a little more. I still have doubts. I still have fear. But Leo's right. Strength isn't about feeling strong. It's about whether or not you let the fear win. The guilt and self-doubt I felt before was just as much a threat as the horde or Constantine himself. Esma's insults, the village we lost—I refuse to let those things take me down.

I'll fight—until my last breath, with my whole heart—to save the people I love.

13

ARIES

The next few days are filled with bouts in the training ring, strategy sessions, and reviewing reports from the front lines. I don't even have a chance to corner my mother to ask her about the blight she's been fending off alone all this time. So far, no one else has reported signs of it, and I can only hope whatever threat it harbors is one that can wait—at least until after we deal with the orc army.

At night, Leo and I patrol the skies, checking the horde's progress through the mountains and looking for weak spots in their lines.

They're a hell of a lot closer than they were yesterday, Leo says when we finally spot their camp many miles from where it was last night.

Too close, I snarl back at him.

My mood has deteriorated these last few days, thanks to a grueling schedule and little time with Paige. She's gone nearly as long as I am each day, rising early and hurrying off alone to wander the grounds. At night, when we both return to bed, exhaustion is etched into her beautiful face. She won't offer details of her activities, and I've resisted the urge to pry. At least, the guilt and sorrow have lifted. In its place is an unyielding determination. A strength that's bone-deep and unmoving in the face of this war.

It's that strength I cling to now, especially as I note how much progress the horde has made into our lands.

They'll be in Misthaven by end of week, Leo says grimly.

I don't answer, but we both know what that means. The front lines we thought would hold them back have failed.

We fly onward, and soon enough, my fears are confirmed. The evidence of a bloody battle lies scattered in the small valley below. Even from way up here, I can see there are no survivors.

My stomach churns, and my dragon's belly burns with rage for the lives lost here today. I turn sharply, doubling back for the horde's camp.

Whoa, brother, what are you doing? Leo calls from behind me.

Soaring within range of the orc camp, I scan the ground for any scouts who might have spotted us already. But no one calls out as the rest of the camp sleeps.

It's time to fight with fire, I tell him.

He doesn't argue or even ask what I mean. We both know it's time to let them see what Astronia's royal dragons can do.

We torch six of their transport carts before they rally and begin firing back at us, screaming their outrage into the night.

They rally quickly.

Gunpowder laces the air as bullets whizz past dangerously close to our wings. Leo's close on my heels as we retreat, and I breathe a sigh once I know he's escaped unharmed. The damage we caused the orcs tonight isn't nearly enough to stop them, but hopefully, it'll slow them down.

We're out of time to train and prepare.

The enemy is nearly on our doorstep, and if we don't go out to meet it, we'll only delay the inevitable. Ready or not, the Astronian army must fight.

The next morning, I call a meeting in the council's chambers. My captains arrive first. Then Blossom and Mag. Leo escorts Paige and my mother from where they apparently had breakfast together. Bingo trails behind them all.

Paige comes up beside me, squeezing my hand.

I haven't told her about what happened last night. Partly out of a wish to spare her but mostly because there hasn't been time. I spent the night sending the appropriate requests to the council for permission to march with the army. Their approval has yet to arrive, but there's no time to waste while they play their stupid power games.

I'm moving forward with or without their response.

"Hey, you okay?" Paige asks quietly while everyone takes their seats.

"I'm fine," I assure her though the words are empty and we both know it.

She doesn't press for more, though, and I'm about to call the meeting to order when two more guests arrive. Myantha and Thorne pause in the doorway as every eye turns toward them. I tense as the two council members scan the faces present until they land on me.

"This is a closed meeting for the army," I tell them. "We're simply using the space."

"As is your right as general," Thorne says, managing to sound both deferential and dickish as he comes forward.

"And we're sitting in to observe," Myantha adds, pulling out a chair at the far end of the table. "As is our right as council."

My mother and Leo exchange a glance. Neither of them protests the intrusion though I know they want to.

"Does this mean you've made your decision?" I ask, hating the fact that those words must leave my mouth at all.

“The army is yours to command,” Thorne says, irritation flashing in his eyes. “The decision to march lies with you.”

His words are gracious enough on the surface, but I know better than to relax just yet. They wouldn’t have come without an agenda.

“Does that decision-making extend to whom I allow in my meetings?” I ask.

Thorne smiles. “It does. Though I wonder why you wouldn’t want a witness to be present for a strategy session that could so easily be misquoted against you later.”

“Who would—” I bite back a snarl as understanding dawns.

Esma.

Then again, it could just as easily be Thorne himself at this point.

I glance at Myantha, who meets my gaze steadily before offering a slight dip of her chin. I can only hope that gesture means she’s a true ally here and not someone who would back-stab me for my crown when the moment arrives.

“In that case, let’s begin,” I say, forcing myself to focus on the task at hand.

The sooner I win this war, the sooner I can regain my throne. First order as king—exile the traitorous council members.

With a furious nod at Leo, I step back as he pushes to his feet and points to the map in the center of the table.

“This map reflects the horde’s updated location,” Leo begins.

All eyes turn to the map and the carefully placed miniatures that represent the orcs.

“Wait. That’s on this side of the mountain range,” my mother says.

I nod. “Yes. They’ve broken through our lines and made it across the valley.”

“They’re dangerously close to Misthaven,” Myantha says, concern lacing her words.

"Within a day's march," Leo says grimly. "Aries and I did what we could to slow them down."

"Whoa. Hang on. What did you do?" Paige asks.

"We torched some of their ammunition carts," I say without looking over at her.

"And I'm guessing, to do that, you had to get within range of their retaliation," she says flatly.

I glance over to see her glaring at me with arms crossed. Damn. I knew this was coming. "We were careful—"

"Did you inform anyone that you were launching an air strike?" she presses.

The room is utterly silent.

"We had to slow them down to give us time to reach the village before they did," I tell her quietly.

She huffs but doesn't argue. I exhale, relieved it wasn't worse. Through the mate bond, I send silent reassurance. It's met with grudging acceptance, and I have to bite back a smile at that.

Finally, I look back at Leo just in time to see him smother a grin before he goes back to the map.

"As you can see," he says, "the horde is far too close to Misthaven, which is a valuable stronghold for us."

"Are there civilians in that village?" Blossom asks.

"Great question." Leo swings his gaze to Myantha and Thorne. "I think the council has been handling those matters until recently."

Thorne meets my brother's stare coldly. "Yes," he answers. "At last report, there are still civilians in Misthaven."

"You haven't evacuated?" Paige asks sharply.

Thorne turns to her, his assessing sweep meant as an obvious insult. "Not to my knowledge."

"Why not?" Paige demands.

Thorne clears his throat. "I'm not sure you're cleared for that kind of classified information."

I start to respond, but Paige cuts me off. "Last I checked, I was the only one of us who Aries actually invited to this meeting. So, you tell me who's cleared."

The silence from earlier is nothing compared to the stillness that follows her retort. Thorne's face flushes. It might have been funny watching him get put in his place by another, but considering he holds all the cards to my future, I don't laugh.

"Evacuating civilians or sending extra soldiers in to protect them would only signal to the horde that this location is significant to us. We can't afford for them to find our weapons cache."

"You prioritize weapons over your people's lives?" Paige doesn't wait for an answer before she adds, "We need to send word to evacuate the civilians. Now."

Her words elicit murmurings of agreement from the captains, and my chest swells with pride at the way she's so deftly taken charge.

Leo clears his throat. He gives Paige a slight nod, and she exhales before he goes on, "As much as it pains me to say this, Thorne's not completely wrong. The blacksmith in Misthaven is our most valuable forge. Nearly half our army's weapons are made there."

"Why aren't we already protecting it better if it's so important?" Paige asks.

Leo snorts. "Good question."

Again, he tosses a pointed look at Thorne and Myantha.

Thorne looks ready to explode, but Myantha answers calmly and almost friendly compared to Thorne's dismissal of my mate's questions. "The forge is a well-kept secret," Myantha tells her. "Our best strategy has always been to make sure no one else knows of its existence or its value to us."

"So, they aren't targeting it on purpose then?" Blossom asks.

"No," Myantha says. "But once they realize what's there, I'm sure they'll waste no time either destroying it or taking it for their own."

“Orcs can’t use our weapons,” Thorne snorts. “Their arm span is way too short for our swords.”

“Maybe not, but they can use the forge to make their own,” I say.

Thorne looks pissed enough at my argument, but we both know I’m right.

“The fact is, if the horde takes Misthaven, we’ll be in a tenuous position,” Leo intervenes.

“And if we defeat them,” Mag says, looking between Leo and myself. “Could it turn the tide in our favor?”

Leo and I share a look. “We’d have to decimate their forces and destroy their siege weapons,” my brother says. “That’s a lot to ask from one battle.”

“I’ve done more with less,” Mag says with a confident shrug.

Maybe it’s his careless confidence or the reminder of our hunts together and the things we faced in those worlds, but an idea I’ve been toying with suddenly strikes me as possible.

I lean forward, focusing on the skilled fighters assembled before me. “The forge isn’t the only significant location here. You’re forgetting about the valley.”

“What valley?” Mag asks.

“Here.” Leo points to the section of flat green space just before the village.

“Why is a valley significant?” Mag asks, studying it shrewdly.

“Since this map was made, there have been multiple landslides in that area, shrinking the valley to a narrow passage. The orcs will be forced to slow down to pass through.”

“A bottleneck,” Mag says, slowly nodding.

“We could be waiting for them,” Blossom says, eyes gleaming as she studies the map. “Ambush and trap them.”

“Precisely.” I glance from Mag and Blossom to Paige. “But we’ll be dealing with their … siege weapons up close.”

“I think I can help with that,” Paige says.

I look over at her in pleasant surprise. "You've made progress on our birdhouse idea?"

But Thorne's voice slices through the tension like a blade. "Is this what we're reduced to?" His tone is sharp, laced with contempt. "Relying on outsiders and their… tricks to save a kingdom that has stood on its own for centuries?"

Paige's eyes narrow, and she steps forward, holding Thorne's gaze without a hint of hesitation. "My 'tricks' have kept me and my friends alive through some pretty dark shit. You don't have to like it, but you will respect it."

Thorne's lip curls, but Paige doesn't back down. Instead, she holds his gaze steadily, her voice low and measured. "I've seen what happens when arrogance leads the charge. It gets people killed. So don't expect me to stand by and watch you throw away the lives of everyone in this kingdom because you can't admit when you're wrong."

For a moment, the tension between them crackles like a live wire. Thorne's gaze hardens, his jaw clenched. The room feels like it's holding its breath, waiting for one of them to break.

Finally, Thorne answers, a muscle ticking in his jaw. "I'll send a message to Misthaven for civilian evacuation. But make no mistake, girl—if this fails, if your magic can't help win this war, Aries' crown will be lost. And when that happens, there won't be a throne left for you to cozy up to."

Paige doesn't flinch. Her gaze remains locked on Thorne, and there's a quiet strength in her voice when she responds. "If we fail, it won't matter who sits on the throne. Astronia will fall. But if we succeed, it'll be because we all did our part. Even you."

Thorne's eyes flicker with something—maybe respect, maybe anger—before he turns away, dismissing the conversation with a sharp gesture. "Then we have our strategy," he says. "Let's hope you're not marching to your doom."

I wrap up the meeting with orders for each unit leader.

The room begins to stir as the others murmur amongst themselves, preparing to act on the plan. But the weight of Thorne's words lingers, a stark reminder that failure isn't just an option—it's the end.

I glance at Paige, who meets my eyes with a look that's all business. In this moment, I appreciate whatever inner strength she's found that allows her to stand so sure and firm in the face of doubt.

It's more than a royal skill she's mastered; it's exactly what I need to bolster my own belief. But the specter of Thorne's warning hangs over me like a shadow: If I lose this battle, I lose everything.

What good is a crown without a kingdom to serve?

14

PAIGE

As soon as the council room clears, the weight of what just happened starts to settle in my chest. I can feel the tension radiating from Aries beside me, his thoughts clearly tangled in battle strategies and the heavy burden of leadership. I don't blame him—my mind is whirling too, grappling with everything we've just discussed. The orcs are coming, and if we're not ready, it won't just be our lives on the line—it'll be the future of this entire kingdom.

I glance at Aries, who's still staring at the door, his brow furrowed. I reach out and touch his arm, my fingers curling around his biceps, and he turns to me, the worry in his eyes making my heart ache.

"Hey," I say softly, waiting until his gaze meets mine. "We're going to get through this."

He gives me a tight smile, but it doesn't reach his eyes. "We have to," he replies, his voice low and full of tension. "There's too much riding on this."

I can hear the weight in his words, the responsibility that's crushing him, and I wish I could lift it, even just a little.

"I hope I didn't overstep," I say. "With Thorne, I mean."

"Are you kidding?" The ghost of a smile blooms on his face. "That was worth allowing him into the meeting in the first place."

I smile, but it's short-lived as I take in the haggard lines and dark circles that mark his lack of sleep. He's been gone long into the night these last few days—longer than me even.

I still haven't had a chance to tell him the full extent of my magic's capabilities—a discovery that's finally come after grueling hours of practice and stubborn determination.

"What was that between you and Leo?" he asks, breaking into my thoughts. "It looked as if you were having some silent conversation."

"He found me in the gardens a few days ago," I say. "Right after we returned from seeing that village destroyed. He helped me find strength and hope."

"Whatever he said to you, I'm glad for it, then." He brushes my cheek, his eyes intent on mine though I can sense his distraction. His restlessness.

The battle plan has been decided. And it's as if Aries is already gone, marching to war, though his body remains before me.

"You should get some rest," I tell him gently.

His expression hardens, and I can see the argument in his eyes already.

But then, an idea takes root in my mind, one that's been nagging at me since we first talked about the orcs and Constantine.

"Before you do, I've been thinking," I begin cautiously, "about another way I can help."

His brow furrows again, but there's curiosity there too. "What do you mean?"

I take a deep breath, knowing this is a gamble. But if it works, it could be the answer to all of this. "I think I need to go back. To the library."

The change in him is immediate. Aries stiffens, his eyes narrowing as he shakes his head, but I press on before he can shut me down completely.

"Just hear me out," I say quickly. "Constantine is too confident, Aries. He's got something up his sleeve, and I think it's another way into this world. Another book, another portal—something. If I can get back into the library and find it, I can take it from him. Cut off his access to Astronia, and then we'll be safe. The orcs will still be a problem, but at least we won't have to worry about him sneaking in and out whenever he wants."

"No." His voice is sharp, final. He pulls back slightly, putting space between us, and the coldness of it makes my chest tighten. "It's too dangerous, Paige. I won't let you risk it."

"Think about it," I argue, my frustration rising. "If Constantine has another way in, it doesn't matter how well we fight the orcs—he'll find a way to undermine us, to make everything we do meaningless. We have to stop him at the source."

"No," he repeats, more forcefully this time. "You don't understand. Going back to the library means walking straight into his trap. He's probably waiting for you, hoping you'll do exactly this. And if he catches you—"

"He won't catch me," I insist, my voice rising. "I know that place better than anyone. I can get in and out before he even knows I'm there. Aries, this is our best shot."

He stares at me, his expression hardening into something that feels like stone. "I said no, Paige. I won't lose you to him, especially for something so reckless."

"You think I'm just going to waltz in there without a plan? I'm trying to save us, Aries. Save *you*."

"You're not saving anyone if you get yourself killed," he snaps back. "Or worse, captured. I can't—" He stops himself, taking a breath as if he's trying to rein in his emotions. "I can't let you do this, Paige. It's not just your life on the line. It's mine too. The kingdom's. If you're gone, if Constantine gets his hands on you, we're finished."

The air between us feels heavy, charged with everything we're not saying. I take a step back, my chest tightening with the realization that this is a wall I'm not going to break through. Not now, at least.

"So that's it?" I say, my voice quieter now, but no less tense. "You're just going to shut me down? Not even consider it?"

He looks at me, and for a moment, I see the struggle in his eyes, the conflict between what he wants and what he thinks is right. But then he shakes his head, and his exhaustion deepens to something that goes beyond lack of sleep.

"I'm not trying to control you, Paige. And this isn't…I don't get to decide anything for you. Your choices are your own. I'm saying no because I want to do this together like we promised—but not because of that promise. Because we're better that way. As a team. And the fact is I can't get behind a mission like that right now. Not before the battle with the horde."

By the time he's done talking, I can see the fear and worry right there at the surface, and my frustration lessens just a little bit. I know how he feels. The idea of losing him is just… exactly why I want to do this.

"All right," I say, the word clipped.

Waiting might be the more cautious choice, but it doesn't ease the urgency and drive inside me to *do* something. I turn away from him, my heart pounding in my chest, and start toward the door.

"Paige, wait—" he begins, but I don't stop. I can't. Not when everything inside me feels like it's unraveling.

"It's fine," I say over my shoulder, my voice tight. He starts to respond, but I cut him off. "We have a battle to prepare for. Let's focus on that."

And then I'm out the door, a knot of frustration and fear

tightening in my chest. I know he's trying to protect me, but all I can feel right now is the sting of inaction.

As I make my way down the corridor, I can't help but wonder if facing the horde will be enough or if Constantine has something much more terrible waiting for us on that battlefield than an army of orcs with guns.

WHAT SHOULD BE HALF A DAY'S RIDE TO MISTHAVEN IS A TWO-day march. Considering all the men and supplies in our convoy, Aries says we're making good time, but I can't help the impatience at our slow pace. Anything could happen in two days. The orcs could speed up. Fix their carts. Beat us there and destroy the place before the evacuations are complete. But there's nothing we can do to go any faster.

So we march.

Aries is distant.

Even at night, when we spread our bedrolls out under the stars, he and Leo wait until the camp is settled before leaving for a recon flight with a couple of raven shifters. Even though I know it's for good reason, his absence stings.

We've barely spoken since we left the castle. He's angry at me, I can tell. Maybe even scared. I don't blame him; there's so much at stake for us. But I'm not going to apologize when there's so much riding on this.

Eventually, I drift off alone beneath our blankets.

During the night, I stir when Aries returns and lies down beside me, but in the morning when I wake again, he's already gone. While Aries and Leo lead the march, I fall back and walk with Blossom and Mag instead.

"Hey," Blossom calls.

"Hey," I return, unable to stifle the sigh that follows.

They share a look, and Mag says something about checking

in with Aries. Then he's gone, jogging toward the front with the princes and leaving us alone.

"Subtle," I say.

Blossom smirks. "Mag has never been accused of that in his life."

"Fair point," I say.

We walk in silence before Blossom speaks up. "So, do you want to talk about it?"

"Talk about what?"

She rolls her eyes. "Did you really come back here to hide from your man and pretend nothing is wrong?"

"I'm not hiding," I protest. But at her withering look, I groan. "Fine. I'm taking some space. Not hiding."

She shakes her head. "You know he's just stressed, right?"

I bite back the retort that bubbles up. Mostly because the soldiers marching around us are ignoring us pointedly—which means they're all listening in to this entire exchange.

My pace slows, and I steer Blossom out of line where we veer farther off from the rest of the men.

"I want to try to make a portal," I say quietly when we're out of earshot.

"A portal to where?" Blossom asks.

"The library."

She stops walking and pulls me around to face her. "Now?"

"Chill," I say, tugging on her until we're both marching forward again.

"Why in the hell would you want to do that—especially right now?" she hisses.

"Because Constantine is feeding off this world, which means he already has another way in. Even if we stop the orcs, Astronia is dying."

"How exactly do you plan to fight him *and* the orcs?"

"I don't want to fight him," I say. "He won't even know I'm

there. I just need to sneak in long enough to find the source of his portal to this world and steal it."

"Paige, that place is crawling with creatures, remember? There is no sneaking in."

I huff. "Whose side are you on?"

"The side of you not getting killed."

"Says the girl currently marching with me into an orc battle."

"Look, I want to save the library just as much as you do. Hell, I get what's at stake if we don't. But we need to be smart. Constantine had years to plan his takeover. We've had days. Aries just wants you both to make it through this to the other side. I can't blame him for being cautious. I would say the same thing if it were Mag."

Her gaze travels the length of the line of men to where Mag walks along beside Aries and Leo. I don't miss the way her expression softens at the sight of him. Mostly because Blossom never used to soften for anyone.

"You really love him, huh?" I ask.

"Don't be ridiculous." She scoffs, but it's so fake I roll my eyes.

"Okay, now who's lying," I say, hip-bumping her.

She snickers, but when she doesn't answer me, I know better than to press it.

We march along in silence for several minutes. Around us, the men talk and laugh. It's hard to imagine we're marching to a bloody battle with the sun shining and spirits so high. Or it would be if I couldn't feel my mate's struggle through our bond. The weight of all he's carrying pressing down around him.

From here, I see Aries doing his best to appear unconcerned despite the swirling of fear inside him. Blossom is right. He's just looking out for me, and I can't fault him for it. I just hope we aren't making a mistake by ignoring the threat Constantine poses.

Beside me, Blossom clears her throat. When she speaks, her

words are so quiet I almost miss them entirely. "You know…. dragons aren't the only shifters to have fated mates."

I stop short, gaping at her. "Wait. Do you mean…"

"Mag is my mate, yes."

Her words strike me speechless.

This time, she's the one to tug me along. I let her, still reeling at her confession. If Mag is her mate, that means… all these years, she's known it and done nothing about it.

"Why did you fight it for so long?" I ask.

"Because I didn't *want* him to be my mate," she says, frustration leaking into her voice. "You know Mag. You knew how he acted, how he would flirt with everyone. Every skirt that walked into the library, he would sidle right up to her."

"But did he know?"

Blossom laughs, but there's more pain than humor in the sound. "No."

My heart pangs at the way she's clearly kept herself so closed off for so long. "He's different when he talks about you, Blossom. He might joke around and flirt with others, but it was only ever to get your attention. To get under your skin. He loves you."

"I think it's taken me a while to believe that," she says. "A long while."

"I knew you were stubborn, but this is just ridiculous," I tease.

She shoves me lightly, laughing as her eyes light up. "I just realized something."

"What is it?"

"Out of all the criminals across all the worlds, the library chose Mag and me as its Keepers. Almost like it wanted us to find each other. And you… Out of all the books you could have accidentally opened, it was this one. It was Aries."

My eyes widen as I realize her point. "Holy shit. Athenaeum is a matchmaker."

Blossom and I share a look, and then we both start laughing.

"Wait until Mag and Aries hear this," I tell her.

"Whoa." She grips my arm, her smile vanishing. "I haven't told him."

"You haven't told him you two are mates?"

"No."

"Why not?"

"I was going to after he was injured in the cavern, but then Constantine showed up, and it was just chaos."

"But we've been here for days now," I say.

"Preparing for war." She shakes her head, all traces of humor gone. "If I don't make it… It would be better this way, for him not to know."

"You should tell him that you love him at the very least," I say. "Before the battle."

She shakes her head. "In case I die—"

"You won't!"

"Paige, it's my choice.

I sigh. She's right. "Fine. But you're telling him after. Promise me. You deserve happiness, Blossom. You both do. Promise me you'll tell him the truth and live happily ever after together."

"I'm not one of your romance novels, you know," she says darkly.

"Oh, you're way more badass than those romance heroines." I lower my voice to a whisper before adding, "Besides, I've had mate sex, and it's honestly so much better than the books let on."

15

ARIES

After doing a quick flyover, I return to the ground and watch the army set up camp following my orders. No talking, no fires, no loud noises. The only space big enough for camp is the hillside that overlooks the village from the south. It's more exposed than I'd like but anything farther, and we won't have the access we need to be ready for them in the morning.

Directly north, on the other side of the valley, the orcs approach. From the looks of it, they will attack at first light, though I haven't dismissed the possibility of a midnight assault. None of our scouts are capable of getting close enough to know for sure. Not without risking detection.

We'll just have to be ready for anything.

Leo appears at my tent, his sword buckled to his hip. "Camp is set," he says. "We're doing cold rations tonight and tomorrow morning. Anything else?"

"The men need to be battle-ready," I say. "They sleep with their weapons and armor beside them."

"You think the horde will attack before dawn?"

"I think we should be ready just in case."

He nods and starts for the door. “Leo,” I call.

He turns back.

“Whatever happens tomorrow—”

“Don’t.” His expression hardens, and he shakes his head. “We’re not doing goodbye, brother. It’s just one battle.”

I nod, my throat tight because, despite the logic of his words, I can’t shake Mag’s earlier prediction: that this battle could be it. Win or lose, this battle will determine our future—and our survival.

But Leo’s expression is unmoved.

“All right then,” I say hoarsely. “Sleep well, brother.”

“And you,” he says, and then he’s gone, leaving me to track down my mate. Paige has kept her distance lately—but then, so have I. And I refuse to let things remain this way if we’re to march to battle in a few hours—regardless of Leo’s claim that this isn’t goodbye.

I find her helping to distribute cold rations.

I wait patiently, watching her interact easily with the soldiers. It’s clear from their easy way with her that they’ve already accepted her as one of us. Seeing it makes my heart swell with gratitude.

When this is over, she’ll be their queen. But she’s already their leader in all the ways that count.

Finally, she finishes up and catches my eye, approaching slowly. I can’t blame her. I’d be wary, too, after how we left things.

“Do you need me for another task?” she asks.

I step closer, reaching out to tuck her hair behind her ear. “I always need you, love.”

My words and touch are soft, but she doesn’t relax. This will be harder than I thought. “I’m going over tomorrow’s strategy one last time. Join me?”

She frowns, unmoved.

I sigh. "I'm sorry. For how I behaved before. The thought of you in harm's way terrified me, and I reacted badly."

"I understand being scared. I worry about you too," she says. "But we can't avoid risk. Constantine is coming whether we want to face it or not."

"I agree. Sooner rather than later, I'm afraid."

Worry lines crease her forehead. "Do you think he'll show up? Tomorrow, I mean."

"He thrives on chaos, and I think he's had his hand in this since the beginning, so I think we need to be ready for that possibility. It's why I want to go over things with you."

She bites her lip, nodding. "Okay."

We return to our tent, neither one of us speaking until the flap closes behind us.

Inside the tent, the air feels heavy with the weight of unspoken words. The flickering light from a single lantern casts shadows across the canvas walls, creating an intimate atmosphere despite the impending battle.

I spread the map out on the table between us, pointing to the positions we've set.

"Here," I say, tapping the area where the orc forces are likely to strike first. "This is the most vulnerable point. We've dug ditches all the way around this area so the orcs won't be able to bring their guns close enough to assault the village itself, but if their soldiers break through our line, it could split our forces and cut off any retreat."

Paige nods, her focus sharpening as she leans closer to study the map. "We'll need to reinforce this area," she says, her voice steady. "Maybe move some of the archers here, behind the front lines, to provide cover."

"I agree," I say, tracing a line with my finger. "And if Constantine does show up…"

"We'll need a plan to deal with him," she finishes for me.

"We don't have enough men to fight two enemies," I say,

voicing the thing that's worried me all along. Not to mention Astronian soldiers don't stand a chance against a creature like Constantine.

Paige's expression tightens with worry. "If anything happens, I can create a portal to get the others out of here."

"What about you?" I can't help but ask.

The moment the words are out, I brace myself for her anger. She's tired of me trying to shield her, yet here I am doing it again. But her eyes soften, and she reaches out to take my hand, her touch grounding me in a way nothing else can.

"I want to show you something," she says.

It's not what I'm expecting.

She releases my hand, stepping back a bit. There's a beat of silence where nothing happens. A second later, a stone wall appears between us nearly as tall as our heads.

I stare at it, stunned. "What…"

Paige laughs. "Touch it."

I press my palm to its surface and find it solid. Not a glamour or trick then.

"How?" I ask.

In answer, the stones separate from one another, cleaving away from the mortar that holds them together. Before my eyes, they explode into dust. I step back, shielding myself from the small explosions, but there's no need. The stone wall vanishes again, leaving only empty space.

Paige shrugs at me. "I've been practicing."

She takes a step toward me, her eyes shining. "I can protect myself, Aries. And others, if it comes to that."

My chest loosens where fear had tightened it. There are no guarantees, of course, but seeing her become so adept at her magic is a comfort. It's also another weapon in our arsenal.

"How does it work?" I ask.

Her forehead scrunches. "I'm not sure exactly, but I think I'm just borrowing from the past."

"The past?" My brows lift. "Do you time travel now?"

She laughs. "No, but I think my magic sort of does." At my look of confusion, she explains, "When Constantine pulled me into that memory and I saw myself restore my home world after he destroyed it, it was obvious what I created was a past version of that world. The homes and structures were outdated, clearly from a time long ago. Then, in the garden that day, I reduced your birdhouse to the wood splinters it came from."

I smile ruefully but then remember the birdhouse wasn't the only casualty. "And the tree?"

"Trying to recreate a life—any life—won't work," she says quietly. "That sort of energy isn't mine to manipulate. When I tried… it only became distorted."

"So, only objects with no life force then."

"I'm sure there's a crossover somewhere," she says, frowning as if in thought. "The wood used to restore the houses and farms was once a living tree…but yes. More or less. Anyway, after the birdhouse and the tree, I realized I wasn't creating something from nothing. I was *re*-creating. Once I understood that, it became easier to wield my magic. And because of that, I think I know a way to render their siege weapons useless."

Hope surges inside me. "How?"

She shrugs. "That metal was raw and unformed once. So it can be again."

"Paige, that's brilliant. And the portal?"

"I think it's sort of the same principle," she says. "Recreating portals that have been made in the past. It feels like… everything that's ever been created before now exists somewhere in the unseen. And my magic is simply pulling it off some invisible shelf for re-use."

"You are a miracle," I tell her, awed by what and who she is.

She presses her palms to my chest, her gaze full of the determination I feel. "We're going to win. Not just tomorrow's fight but the war. And then we're going to get your crown back."

"I'm sorry for pushing you away," I say, grabbing her waist and pulling her close. "I was afraid of losing you. I can't do this without you."

"I'm right here, and I'm not going anywhere," she whispers.

Our gazes hold, and the tension between us shifts, crackling with an undercurrent of need. We both know what's at stake, but right now, the weight of tomorrow only fuels the urgency between us.

I close the distance, seizing her lips in a hungry kiss. There's nothing tender about it—just raw desire, the kind that's been building for days, intensified by the thought of what's to come. My hands move to her waist, pulling her against me with a force that makes her gasp into my mouth.

The sound elicits a growl from deep within me.

Paige responds in kind, her fingers digging into my shoulders as she presses herself against me, meeting my urgency with her own. There's no hesitation, no holding back. The need to feel her, to taste her, drowns out everything else.

I back her up against the table, our bodies colliding with a mix of desperation and devotion. The map crumples beneath her as I lift her onto the table's edge, her legs wrapping around my waist, pulling me closer. I can feel the heat of her through our clothes, the friction driving me wild as I grind against her.

She tugs at my shirt, her breath coming in short, heated bursts as she works to get it off. I help her, yanking the tunic over my head and tossing it aside. Her hands are on me immediately, exploring the planes of my chest, her nails scraping lightly over my skin.

"Fuck," I growl against her lips, the sensation sending a jolt of pleasure straight to my cock.

I tear at her clothes, pulling her shirt off and tossing it aside, revealing the smooth, bare skin beneath. My mouth is on her neck in an instant, teeth grazing her pulse before I suck hard, marking her as mine. Her moan only spurs me on, the sound low and throaty—a plea for more.

Her hands are frantic as they move down to the waistband of my pants, her fingers brushing against the hard length straining against the fabric. I groan, the sound primal, as she strokes me through the material, her touch driving me to the edge of control.

"Aries," she whispers. Commanding me. Begging me.

I don't need to be told twice. I unbuckle my pants and shove them down, freeing myself as I lean back to take in the sight of her—flushed, panting, her eyes dark with desire.

My control snaps.

I yank her pants off, pulling them down her legs and tossing them aside in one swift motion.

She's bare before me, her skin glowing in the dim light, and I'm on her in an instant, my mouth crashing against hers as I position myself between her legs.

There's no gentleness, no slow build-up. I enter her in one powerful thrust, burying myself to the hilt.

"Fuck," she gasps, her back arching as her nails dig into my back.

The feeling of her, tight and slick around me, nearly undoes me, but I hold on, setting a hard, relentless pace. Every thrust is rough, desperate, fueled by the need to claim her, to lose ourselves in each other before the chaos of tomorrow.

Paige meets me with equal intensity, her hips lifting to meet every thrust, her breath hot against my ear as she moans. Her hands are everywhere—grasping my shoulders, my back, her nails leaving marks that I'll wear proudly.

"Don't stop," she gasps.

I growl in response, my hand gripping her thigh as I push her harder against the table, angling deeper. The sounds she makes drive me wild—whimpers, gasps, cries of pleasure that mix with the slaps of our bodies colliding.

The tension coils tighter, a hot, electric pulse between us as we push each other closer to the edge. I can feel her tightening around me, her body trembling with the force of her approaching climax.

"Come for me," I command, my voice rough, feral.

Her answer is a wordless cry as she shatters, her body shuddering against me as she tips over the edge. The sight of her, lost in ecstasy, pulls me under, and with a final, powerful thrust, I join her.

We're both panting as the last waves of pleasure ripple through us. I press my forehead to hers, trying to catch my breath, our bodies still connected, sweat-slicked and trembling.

Slowly, I pull back, lifting her off the table and carrying her to the bedroll, laying her down gently. I collapse beside her, pulling her close.

Finally, I break the silence, my voice low, rough. "Whatever happens tomorrow, know that you're mine. I don't need magic to find my way back to you—in every life I get."

She turns her head, capturing my gaze with those bright, glittering eyes. "I love you," she whispers.

I pull her closer, our lips meeting in a final, lingering kiss, this one softer, a promise more than a demand. We stay like that, wrapped around each other, letting the warmth of our bodies lull us into sleep for what might very well be our last night in this life. I dream only of finding her in the next.

16

PAIGE

Beside me, Aries sleeps soundly. I don't blame him. Whatever nervous energy we had was spent earlier. I'm not sure why I'm wide awake now, considering my own exhaustion before, but as I lay beside him in our tent, my mind whirs and I know sleep isn't happening anytime soon.

Giving up, I climb quietly out of bed and pull on my clothes before slipping outside. The camp is fully dark as I wander through the maze of tents. The only soldiers still awake are the ones standing guard or patrolling the perimeter. I nod at a couple of them and earn a quick smile from each.

I've made it nearly to the edge of camp when I see a figure sitting on a fallen log. They aren't wearing a soldier's uniform. Worried, I creep closer until I can make out their shape and features.

It's not only her height and build that give her away. It's that blonde ponytail glowing in the moonlight that makes her unmistakable.

I approach Blossom quietly, not wanting to disturb her if she's deep in thought, but she looks up and catches my eye before I can decide whether to interrupt.

"Can't sleep?" she asks, her voice low but warm. She gestures for me to join her.

I sit down beside her. "Too much on my mind, I guess."

She nods, understanding without me needing to say more. "It's always like this before a big fight. You start thinking about all the 'what ifs,' and they just won't let you rest."

"Yeah," I admit, staring up at the stars winking back at us. "I used to lay awake at night, worrying about all of my Head Librarian duties—and that was mostly just paperwork." She snorts. I smile, but it vanishes quickly. "The stakes are a lot higher this time around."

"You're worried about Constantine showing up."

"You've thought about it too?"

"Of course. I'd be naïve not to consider it. Especially since he's already been here to supply our enemies with weapons."

I blow out a breath. "I don't know if I'm ready to face him."

"Please. He's terrified of you. You just have to figure out why."

"He's got a funny way of showing fear—taking over the library and nearly killing us and all."

"He's relentless in his pursuit of you, Paige."

"Yeah, because he's psycho and obsessed."

"Maybe, but I think he knows you're the one who can stop him."

I scowl. "I wish I knew it, too. Or how to actually do it."

"You'll figure it out. You always do."

"Sometimes your blind faith in me is really annoying."

She grins back at me, the usual mischief in her eyes tempered by something softer. "Someone's got to hype you up, right? Who better than a best friend?"

I laugh, the sound more genuine than I expected. "Yeah, I guess so."

For a while, we just sit there, the fire crackling between us, sharing the quiet comfort of each other's presence. The fear is still there, but it's manageable now, tempered by the knowledge that I'm not facing this alone.

Eventually, Blossom speaks again, her words quiet. "Hoc would be proud of you, you know."

I swallow past the lump in my throat, the weight of her words settling over me like a blanket. "Thanks. That really means a lot."

She nods, and then her expression shifts, a teasing glint returning to her eyes. "That said, if you could avoid getting yourself killed tomorrow, that'd be great. I've grown kind of attached to you."

I chuckle, the tension in my chest easing just a little more. "I'll do my best."

THE FIRST LIGHT OF DAWN FILTERS THROUGH THE TENT, CASTING a pale glow over the fabric walls. I wake slowly, especially after my midnight chat with Blossom. The warmth of Aries' body is still wrapped around mine, his arm draped possessively across my waist. For a brief moment, I let myself savor the quiet, the feel of his skin against mine, the steady rise and fall of his chest as he breathes.

But reality comes crashing back with the distant sound of a horn, its mournful call signaling the start of what I've been dreading. My heart lurches, and the fog of sleep clears instantly, replaced by a sharp, cold awareness.

The battle is upon us.

Aries stirs behind me, pressing a soft kiss to my cheek before he sits up and tosses back the blankets. We dress quickly and quietly and meet at the flap, hesitating there as we lock eyes.

"It's time," I say finally.

He nods, his expression hardening as if a weight is settling over him. There's no more time for words, no more time for anything but what must be done. The intimacy of last night is gone, replaced by the fierce determination in his eyes, the look of a man ready to face death if it means protecting what he loves.

We step out of the tent together, the early morning light casting long shadows across the camp. The hillside is alive with movement, soldiers donning armor, sharpening weapons, their faces set in grim lines as they prepare for the fight of their lives.

I scan the horizon, searching for any sign of the orcs. The valley below is shrouded in mist, the mountains in the distance barely visible through the haze. But I can feel them, a dark presence just beyond the edge of sight, waiting to descend upon us.

"Paige," Aries says, his voice low as he hands me a dagger. "Stay close to me. No matter what happens, we fight together."

I nod, slipping the dagger into my belt, the cool metal reassuring against my hip. "I will."

Leo approaches, his armor gleaming in the early light, sword strapped to his back. He gives us a curt nod, his expression unreadable. "Scouts report movement in the pass. They're coming."

"Are the men in position?" Aries asks.

"Ready and awaiting your orders for the ambush," Leo says.

"Tell them to wait until the front lines spot our advancing army in the valley. They'll fire on my command."

Leo nods. The three of us exchange a look, a silent understanding passing between us. This is it. There's no turning back now.

As we move to join the others, my heart pounds in my chest, the adrenaline already surging through my veins. I've faced danger before, but nothing like this—nothing on this scale. The weight of the responsibility presses down on me, but I push it aside, focusing on the task at hand. There's no room for fear, no room for doubt.

The soldiers on the hillside fall into formation, their eyes locked on Aries as he steps forward, his presence commanding, every inch the leader they need him to be. He raises his sword, the blade catching the light, and for a moment, the world holds its breath.

"Today, we fight for Astronia!" he shouts, his voice ringing out across the hillside. "We fight for our families, for our homes, for everything we hold dear. We fight because we will not let these bastards take what is ours!"

A roar rises from the soldiers, their voices a fierce, unified cry that echoes through the valley. The sound sends a shiver down my spine, and I grip the hilt of my dagger tighter, the resolve solidifying in my chest. This is more than just a battle. It's survival. It's everything.

As the soldiers take their positions, I find my place beside Aries, my magic thrumming just beneath the surface, ready to be unleashed. I can feel the power coursing through me, the energy coiled and waiting like a spring ready to snap. I've never been more aware of it, more in control, and it gives me a sense of calm amid the chaos.

Maintaining our formed lines, we wait on the hillside for what feels like forever. Our army stands in plain sight of the orcs —or we will be the moment they emerge from the narrow pass. But that's part of the ambush. Thinking we're all ready and waiting out here in the open. And when the pass is full of orc soldiers, our archers will attack from the cliffs above.

The ground beneath us trembles as the orc army's front lines emerge from the mist, a dark, seething mass of muscle and steel, their war cries rising like a wave of death. Behind them are large guns mounted to carts, each one dragged along by orc soldiers on wooden wheels far more rudimentary than the gleaming weapons are.

My stomach tightens at the sight of them.

Aries assured us the ditches will prevent them from getting within range, but even so, I begin calling on my magic so I can do my part to render them useless. Before I get that far, movement at the front lines draws my eye.

Our soldiers emerge through the mist, ready for battle. The orcs scream angrily at the sight of the Astronian warriors, the bloodthirsty sound of it sending a shudder through me.

"Fire," Aries roars.

Archers appear along the craggy cliffs, their bows aimed down as they fire their arrows into the crowded pass. Orcs drop by the dozen as the arrows hit their mark.

Up front, the horde charges forward, a tidal force of destruction as our soldiers rush to meet them. The air is suddenly filled with the sound of clashing steel, of screams and shouts, as the two armies collide.

Our vantage point is high enough to remain out of the battle, and I concentrate again on destroying the guns being loaded and aimed. It takes only a moment to awaken the magic inside me. And then only another few to render the first gun into a piece of unformed metal—just as it once had been.

The orcs pulling the weapon stop and scream their shock and outrage.

I turn to Aries, smiling at my victory, but he's frowning down at the battle itself. I follow the direction of his gaze and see Mag and Blossom below us, surrounded by orcs as they defend our hillside.

My breath catches as I realize how close our enemy has gotten.

"Draw your blade," Aries says to me.

I do as he says, fumbling for it as fear takes me over.

But his gaze is steady on mine as he turns to me. "Stay here with Leo," he says, gesturing to where Leo is giving orders to a runner who will deliver them to the archers.

"Be careful," I say around the lump in my throat.

He doesn't answer as he turns and races down the hill.

Aries moves like lightning, his sword a blur as he cuts down orcs left and right. Forcing myself to refocus on my own tasks, I unleash my magic on the guns. One by one, each of them melts into a sheet of unmade metal, much to the orc's outrage.

When those are gone, I scan for Aries and the others, sighing in relief when I see them all spread over the hillside and down into the field below. Aries is covered in blood, but a quick check of the mate bond assures me none of it is his. Mag and Blossom are a force as they cut through orcs together—as if they're doing some sort of tandem dance.

Our other soldiers, however, are not so lucky. Already, the valley is littered with lost lives. My heart squeezes at the sight of so much destruction and death. Too many of the fallen are Astronian—though, I'm determined to stop that number from rising. Drawing on my magic, I use it to create barriers of stone and wood, protecting soldiers from unseen attacks at their flanks.

Time becomes meaningless as the battle rages on, the hours blending into one another, marked only by the rise and fall of enemies, by the surges of power and exhaustion. I lose count of how many soldiers I've protected from a fatal blow—and how many times I wasn't fast enough, the faces of the fallen already blurring in my memory.

Those losses only push me harder, more determined than ever to make my magic count. Eventually, I begin to notice the orc army dwindling.

Relief, elation—victory—surge inside me.

I catch Leo's eye, needing to know. "Are they running?" I ask.

"It seems so," he says, the grimness from earlier replaced by a stark relief. "We'll catch the ones that try. It's over, Paige. We've won."

His words are punctuated by the clang of swords, but the sound of it no longer sparks dread in my veins.

We've won.

Leo's words echo inside me.

Aries puts another orc down and then slowly begins to make his way toward me.

I watch him, grateful and stunned. We made it.

We actually made it out alive.

But then, through the haze of battle, a familiar darkness begins to creep into the edges of my vision. The air grows colder, the light dimmer, as a shadow spreads over the far side of the valley.

It creeps over the grass, rotting it instantly as the shadow surges forward.

The blight is here, but it's more than that.

It's exactly what I feared most.

My magic begins to drain, and I clamp down on its flow, cutting it off from myself—and from him siphoning it away.

Constantine has arrived.

"Paige!" Aries' voice cuts through the din, and I turn to see him staring up at the ridge behind me.

I spin to find a figure cloaked in shadow standing ominously above me, the very air around him warping with his dark magic.

Constantine.

The sight of him sends a bolt of fear through me, but it's quickly followed by a surge of anger, of determination. This is the moment we've been dreading but also the one we've been waiting for.

"Who is that?" Leo asks, at my side instantly.

Aries joins us, out of breath.

"His name is Constantine," I say quietly. "He's from my world."

"What does he want?" Leo asks.

Aries and I exchange a look.

"Me," I say.

"Paige," Aries begins, his tone a warning. But we both know it's no use. The threat is here. We have no choice but to face it.

"We finish this," I say, my voice steady despite the storm raging around us.

Aries nods, his eyes locking with mine, a promise in his gaze. "Together."

We break into a run, cutting our way through the battlefield, the chaos of the fight falling away as our focus narrows to one goal: reaching Constantine. The world around us seems to fade, the noise, the blood, the bodies—none of it matters anymore. All that matters is stopping him.

Constantine watches us approach, his expression unreadable, but I can feel the power radiating from him, a dark, oppressive force that presses down on my chest, making it hard to breathe. But I don't falter. I won't.

"I see your time away from the library has been productive," he says, nodding at the battlefield.

"Your meddling here did nothing to stop us," Aries snarls.

"Is that so, Your Highness? Or does that title no longer apply?"

Aries merely glares at him.

"How did you get here without the book?" I demand—curiosity and worry driving me.

His lips twist smugly. "My time as Head Librarian has been productive as well."

"You can portal without the books," I say.

It's not a question, but Constantine's ego won't let him miss a chance to brag about his capabilities either. "The library's magic, fused with my own, is a powerful doorway. Now, those doors open for me at will. But if you prefer a portal…"

He waves his hand, and a dark, swirling portal opens farther down the hillside. I spot Mag and Blossom leading a group of soldiers toward us, but they stop short at the sight of the portal cutting off their path forward.

No.

Not the portal itself.

The dark and disgusting creatures that pour out of it are a far bigger threat than the doorway between worlds. Even bigger than the orc army we've just defeated.

Hellhounds, basilisks, and a minotaur rush out of the portal onto the battlefield. The soldiers cry out in shock, but Blossom and Mag don't hesitate to slash at the monsters with their swords. The minotaur manages to get inside Blossom's defenses, but Mag shoves his body in front of hers, the blow clanging against Mag's stony exterior. Blossom sweeps in from the side and puts her sword through the minotaur's thigh. It jumps back to avoid another hit but looks ready to try again.

I resist the urge to offer help, knowing it will only give Constantine the meal he so desperately wants.

When I look back at him, he's grinning, proving my suspicions.

My hands curl into fists.

"This ends today," I say.

"Oh yes, little mage," Constantine says, his eyes gleaming as battle cries and clashing swords ring out around us. "I couldn't agree more."

Aries reaches him first, his sword slashing through the air, but Constantine deflects the blow with a wave of his hand, the force of it sending Aries stumbling back. Aries straightens, and we share a look. I nod, and he attacks again. This time, I conjure a shield to take the brunt of Constantine's counter-blow, and Aries manages a swipe that slices into Constantine's arm.

Blood appears in the wound, and I watch, satisfied, as it stains his coat.

With a hiss, Constantine waves his other hand, and an invisible force knocks Aries back again. Then he focuses on me, sucking up my magic as if through a straw. I cut it off as he pauses, his eyes narrowing.

"So, the little mage thinks she can play with the big boys," Constantine sneers, his voice dripping with contempt.

"Let's see if you can keep up," I snap back, raising my hands to go again.

Aries and I move as one, with me on defense and him on offense, each strike designed to push Constantine back, to wear him down. After each defensive maneuver, I yank my magic back to me, turning it off before he can siphon it away. But he's strong—stronger than I anticipated—and he's not just deflecting our blows; he's absorbing them.

A process that only makes him more dangerous, more powerful.

Out of the corner of my eye, I see Blossom and Mag and the other soldiers battling the creatures that pour from the portal. For every monster they take out, more appear.

Shutting down the portal would take more concentration than I can spare, so I focus on Constantine—and Aries' attempts to get past the asshole's shields.

Again and again, we strike and block.

The ground trembles beneath us as our powers clash, the very air crackling with energy. The world narrows to the three of us, the battle fading into the background as we fight for control, for survival.

Aries brings his sword down hard toward Constantine's outstretched arm. The sight of the blade sends Constantine stepping back, and I act fast, creating a large hole in the hillside behind him. His boot hits the ledge, and he tips backward, his balance shifting with his momentum.

My breath catches, but I don't stop there, conjuring a portal at the bottom of the hole. Unlike the one I made to bring us here, this one is remade from all the worst parts of the dark prison worlds Hoc and the other Keepers trained me to avoid at all costs. It's a risk to create it here, now, but we have to do something before his creatures overrun our army.

Or worse, he drains all my magic away.

Even from here, the portal's force whips my hair as it attempts to suck Constantine into its swirling depths.

Fear flashes across his face, and I feel a tug on my magic as he sips on the power flowing through me and into the hole.

I can't afford to stop the flow of magic now. Not when it powers the portal. I grit my teeth, praying I have enough of it left to send him into the darkness before he drains me.

At the last second, Constantine recovers. He steps clear of the hole, and his lips curl into a cruel smile. Dread pools in my stomach as I feel the magic between us shift. It feels as if we're in a tug of war and he just yanked on his end hard enough to send my magic flowing right to him.

"That's better," he says.

With a flick of his wrist, he tears open a portal of his own making just behind Aries, the dark void swirling with ominous energy.

"Let's take this somewhere more…private, shall we?" he says, his voice a dangerous purr.

Before we can react, the portal pulls us in, the world around us twisting and warping as we're sucked into the darkness.

My stomach lurches as the ground falls away, and then we're hurtling through space, the cold, dark magic of the portal surrounding us.

"Paige!" Aries yells my name, the sound of it echoing inside the tunnel.

I try to call out for him, but the sound of my voice is lost to the roar of nothingness.

When we emerge, the ground beneath our feet is hard and familiar. The air is musty, filled with the scent of old parchment and ink. And though it looks vastly different than it did before, I would know this place anywhere.

We've landed inside the Athenaeum.

Just like I knew we would.

17

PAIGE

Aries grips my hand, and we both spin, scanning for Constantine among the stacks. But he's nowhere in sight, and the portal itself is gone—sealing us inside. A chill runs down my spine as I realize we've been cut off from Astronia and the others still fighting there.

Now, it's just me and Aries—and Constantine, wherever he is.

The air in the Athenaeum crackles with tension, thick and oppressive. The once-grand library is now a twisted labyrinth of darkened corridors and malevolent shadows. The walls, lined with books that contain the stories of countless worlds, seem to close in on us, each step forward echoing in the eerie silence.

"I can portal us out," I say quickly. "Back to the battle."

"No." Aries' voice is tight. "If we go back, he'll only follow, and more people will get hurt."

He's right, but fear holds me still.

He tugs on my hand, drawing my gaze to his. "You can do this."

I nod, not trusting my voice.

"Where is he hiding? The cavern?"

I shake my head. "He's close. I can feel it."

"Then let's find him and finish this," Aries snarls, his voice a low growl as his eyes scan the shadows. His dragon is close to the surface; I can feel it through our bond—his anger, his desperation. His rage.

I use it to fuel my own—and to chase away the fear that threatens. Leo's words ring out in my head: It's not about being fearless. It's about facing the threat, anyway.

We make our way slowly.

Constantine's presence is everywhere, his dark magic seeping into the very fabric of the library. The once-vibrant tapestries now hang in tatters, and the shelves, once meticulously organized, are now chaotic with books scattered and torn, their pages fluttering as if caught in an invisible wind.

Some of those pages are blank now.

I try not to think about what that means for the worlds that used to be written there.

The Athenaeum, once a place of knowledge and sanctuary, is now a battlefield.

As much as it makes my heart ache, I force myself to see past the mark Constantine has left on this place—to the memory of what it was before. What it could be again. A protector and keeper of stories. A sanctuary. A beating heart where all the worlds collide and exist as one.

The Athenaeum is more than just a building. Or she was before Constantine invaded her and stole her spirit.

Maybe I can steal it back.

"We need to find the heart of the library," I realize.

"Do you think that's where he went?"

"I don't know, but I have an idea."

Aries frowns, and I know every part of him wants to rush toward the monster, but he nods, trusting me. "Okay, how do we find it?"

I wince. "I'm not sure. I only ever visited there in a vision the library showed me. But I know it's the source of magic for this place. And if he hasn't siphoned it all away, it might give me the boost I need to defeat him."

But Aries doesn't scoff at my answer. He squeezes my hand. "Can you re-create it from your vision? Use your magic to get us inside?"

I nod, swallowing the fear that rises in my throat. "I can try."

Before I get that far, movement has us both whirling.

A blur of black cloak vanishes around the corner of the stacks. Books fly toward us, their pages ruffling as something emerges from inside them. A long, scaly body wraps around my wrist. Aries' sword slashes against it, cutting the snake in two.

It falls to the ground at our feet, still writhing, its viscous blood burning holes in the books it touches. The scent is vile, clogging my nostrils as the blood runs along the floor at our feet.

"Poison," I choke.

"Get back," Aries says, pulling me to safety.

I thrust my magic out, and the blood and snake vanish as I re-create the book back to its original form. A pile of unmarked, unbound paper. Their edges flutter in the wake of the magic's force.

I stare at it, stunned.

"No," I breathe.

"What's wrong?" Aries asks.

He looks left and right, no doubt searching for another threat.

But I'm the only threat standing here now.

Aries eventually glances at me, but I can't answer him. The poison might be gone, but so is the story it came from. An entire world—wiped from existence. Because of me.

Nausea rolls through my stomach.

I swallow, trying not to be sick at the thought of what I've just done.

Constantine's laugh echoes through the darkened halls, a low, sinister sound that sends a chill down my spine. "So brave, little mage," he taunts, his voice seeming to come from everywhere and nowhere at once. "You think you can defeat me? In my own domain?"

Aries looks over at me, his expression blazing with fury.

"Paige, the library's core. Can you get us there?" he asks sharply.

"I think so." My magic hums just beneath my skin, itching to be unleashed, but I'm afraid—afraid of what Constantine might do and afraid of what it might cost to stop him.

Then again, if we do nothing, every one of these books will be empty soon.

I take a deep breath.

My magic swirls to life the moment I call on it.

And just as quickly, I can feel it being drained.

Doing my best to hang on, I use it to recreate my vision of the library's central hub. There's no portal this time, no doorway to step through to take us there. Instead, the stacks around us fade away, replaced with the chamber I remember standing inside with Athenaeum herself.

The day she named me Hoc's successor.

The day she revealed herself to me as the library's spirit.

I blink and look around.

The heart of the library is a vast chamber, its ceiling soaring into darkness. The first time I stood here, everything was lit in bright white, but now gray shadows press in from all sides. In the center of the room is a table. On it lies a massive, ancient tome, glowing with an eerie, pulsating light.

And there, standing before the strange book, is Constantine.

His presence is overwhelming, a dark shadow that seems to suck the little bit of light from the room. His eyes, glowing with a malevolent gleam, fix on me with a hunger that makes my blood run cold.

"You think you can stop me?" he sneers, lifting his hand.

Dark tendrils of magic spiral out from his fingertips, lashing toward me like living snakes.

I barely have time to react. I throw up a barrier, but it shatters under the force of his attack, the impact sending me sprawling to the ground. Pain explodes in my head as I hit the cold, stone floor, and for a moment, everything goes black.

"Paige!" Aries' voice cuts through the haze, filled with panic.

I force myself to sit up, my vision swimming. Constantine's magic presses down on me, suffocating, and I struggle to breathe, to think.

"You are nothing," Constantine hisses, his eyes locked on me as he advances. "A child playing with forces beyond your understanding. Did you really think you could challenge me?"

My heart pounds in my chest, each beat a reminder of how close I am to losing everything. I reach out, trying to draw on my magic, but it feels distant, sluggish, as if Constantine's darkness is sapping it away.

Desperate, I reach for the library's magic, trying to draw from whatever's left. But there's nothing here. Only us and that strange book in the center of it all—pulsing as if alive.

"Get away from her!" Aries roars, and in an instant, he's between us, his body a protective shield. His eyes blaze with fury, the dragon within him barely contained.

Constantine's smile widens, his gaze shifting to Aries. "Ah, the dragon prince stripped of his birthright from his own people. So noble, so foolish." He flicks his wrist, and a wave of dark energy slams into Aries, knocking him back.

"No!" I scream, struggling to my feet. But before I can do anything, Constantine turns his attention back to me, his magic tightening around my throat, lifting me off the ground.

I gasp and kick, clawing at the invisible force choking me, my vision darkening at the edges. Constantine's eyes gleam with sadistic pleasure as he watches me struggle.

"This is the end for you, little mage," he whispers, his voice a deadly promise.

I can feel my strength slipping away, my magic fading as the darkness closes in. I'm going to die here, and there's nothing I can do to stop it.

But then, through the haze of pain and fear, I hear Aries' voice filled with raw, desperate fury. "Let her go!"

Constantine merely laughs.

In the next instant, the entire chamber is engulfed in flames. Aries has unleashed his dragon fire, the intense heat and light searing through the darkness. The flames roar to life, consuming everything in their path.

Constantine's grip on me falters as he reels back, his dark magic retreating in the face of the dragon's fire. I drop to the ground, gasping for breath, as the inferno rages around us.

But the fire is uncontrollable, wild. It spreads across the floor, up the walls. The chamber vanishes, and the library itself returns as the vision I created bleeds away. A mirage only. We never left the stacks. And now, Aries' fire licks across the shelves, lighting the books—incinerating everything.

"No!" I scream, rushing forward, but the flames drive me back again.

The heat singes my clothes, my fingers. The smoke steals my breath, clogging my lungs.

The library is burning, the ancient tomes turning to ash in the flames.

"Aries, stop!" I cry, but he's beyond hearing, his dragon's rage unleashed in full force. I can see the anguish in his eyes, desperation driving him to destroy.

A beam above my head breaks loose, crashing to the ground near my feet.

The library is collapsing around us, the very foundation of the Athenaeum crumbling as the fire consumes it. Constantine, though wheezing, laughs—a chilling sound that echoes through the burning chamber.

"You think fire will stop me?" he sneers, but there's an edge of fear in his voice now, his eyes flickering with uncertainty as the flames close in on him. His shield is weakening.

My magic surges as it returns to me.

He's stopped draining me at last.

This is my chance.

Before I can attack him, another beam falls from the ceiling, this one larger, structural. It crashes down between me and Aries, cutting off my path to him. The heat is unbearable, the flames licking at my skin, and I know that if I don't move, I'll be trapped.

But there's nowhere to go. The fire is everywhere, closing in, suffocating.

And then I see it—a shadow moving through the flames, coming toward me. Constantine's eyes gleam through the smoke, his hand reaching out, and I know that this is it. I'm out of time, out of options.

Just as his fingers brush my skin, everything goes white-hot, and I scream as the world around me explodes in fire and light.

18

ARIES

The flames roar around us, a living, breathing entity of destruction. My dragon fire, once controlled and precise, now rages unchecked, devouring everything in its path. The shelves, the books, the very heart of the Athenaeum—all of it is being consumed by the inferno I've unleashed.

But none of that matters as I watch Constantine move toward Paige.

She's lying on the floor, her body limp and fragile amidst the chaos. Smoke swirls around her, and beneath the smudges of soot on her cheeks, her skin is pale, too pale. My heart thunders in my chest as I realize she's unconscious—vulnerable. And Constantine knows it.

With a wicked grin, he reaches down, his hand glowing with dark magic, ready to take what's left of her for his own—ready to finish what he started.

"No!" I roar, charging forward, but the flames slow me down, the intense heat forcing me to shield my eyes. I swing my sword, sending a wave of fire toward him, but he's faster. He darts to the side, avoiding the flames as he grabs Paige by the arm, pulling her up like she's nothing more than a rag doll.

"Such a waste," he sneers, his eyes glinting with malevolence. "You could have been so powerful, little mage. But now, you'll die like the rest of them."

My fury knows no bounds. The dragon inside me roars, demanding blood, demanding that I tear Constantine apart for daring to touch her.

But I can't get to him—not with Paige in his grasp.

Constantine's grip on her tightens, and I know he's draining her, his magic pulling the life from her soul. Her head lolls to the side, her eyes closed, and a sickening fear grips me. She's not moving. She's not fighting back.

The mate bond flickers.

I have to end this now.

I summon every ounce of power within me, feeling the dragon fire course through my veins. The flames around us intensify, the heat so intense that the very air shimmers with it. The library trembles, the walls cracking under the pressure.

With a final, desperate roar, I hurl myself at Constantine, my sword blazing with dragon fire. I aim for his heart, determined to rip it from his chest.

But he's faster than I expect. He shifts Paige in front of him, using her as a shield. I pull back at the last second, the blade only narrowly missing her flesh as I yank it away.

Constantine laughs, a cold, heartless sound that makes my blood boil. "You can't save her, dragon. You can't save any of them."

Leo was wrong. This is goodbye—and I'm not sure I'll survive it.

Through the bond, I send Paige all my love. The sensation of it is one last, parting embrace. Soul to soul.

It's all I have left to offer, and it's not nearly enough.

But Paige suddenly gasps, her eyes flying open as her breath returns to her body.

Our eyes meet, and then her magic explodes.

Her skin glows with it, and the blinding light forces my eyes shut.

When I open them again, the fire is gone.

Screaming, Constantine stumbles back, his robes smoldering, his skin charred and cracked. Paige falls to the ground, her body free from his grip, but she's still not moving.

"Paige!" I shout, rushing to her side. I drop to my knees, cradling her in my arms.

Her eyes flutter open, and I can see the determination in them, the strength that she's drawing from somewhere deep within. She's not done. Not yet.

"Aries," she whispers, her voice weak but filled with resolve. "Help me stand."

I hesitate, afraid that she's too weak, but she gives me a look that brooks no argument. I help her to her feet, keeping one arm around her waist to steady her.

Constantine appears through the fog, his eyes narrowing as he watches her rise. "Impossible," he hisses, his voice tinged with disbelief. "I drained you of every drop you had."

Paige takes a step forward, her body trembling with effort, but there's a new light in her eyes—a light that blazes with hope, love, and power.

The bond between us thrums with energy, with life. It's not just my power or hers but something greater, something born from the connection we share. A power that Constantine could never understand because it's not about destruction or domination—it's about creation. About love.

The realization hits me like a bolt of lightning. Our bond—it's not just a link between mates. It's a source of magic all its own, a wellspring of light and life that we can draw from when one of us is empty or lost.

"Paige," I say, my voice hoarse with urgency. "Our bond."

She reaches out to me, her hand dark with soot, and I clasp it in mine. The connection between us flares brighter, a golden thread that weaves through the darkness, banishing the shadows, filling the void with warmth and light.

"You've taken enough from me, Constantine," Paige says, her voice gaining strength with every word. "But now, I'm taking it back."

I focus on the love we share, the strength that flows between us, just as I feel Paige doing the same. Constantine recoils, his eyes wide with fear as the light envelops us, growing brighter, stronger with each passing second.

"Love creates," she murmurs, her voice soft but unyielding. "And hate destroys."

With a final, forceful pull, the bond between us explodes into a magic I can feel as if it were my own.

Constantine screams, the sound high-pitched and inhuman, as the light wraps around him, latching onto his stolen magic and ripping it away. He thrashes, trying to break free, but he's no match for the force of creation—of love.

His form begins to wither, the dark energy that once surrounded him dissipating into the air. He shrinks before our eyes, his once-imposing figure now frail and human, his eyes wide with terror as he realizes he's lost.

"No… No, this can't be…" he stammers, his voice weak and broken. He stumbles back, tripping over his own feet, and collapses to the ground, clutching at his chest as if trying to hold on to the last vestiges of his power.

But it's gone. All of it. And without it, Constantine is nothing.

Paige sways, her strength nearly spent, but I catch her before she can fall. The flames around us are gone, but their damage remains. The library is a smoldering ruin of ash and smoke.

Constantine lies at our feet, nothing more than a pitiful, broken man. His eyes, once filled with malice and power, now only reflect fear and despair. The power that once made him so formidable is gone, leaving only a shell of the man who once threatened worlds.

"Please," he begs, his voice barely a whisper. "Don't kill me."

Paige looks down at Constantine, her expression unreadable. She reaches into her belt and withdraws the dagger I gave her this morning before the battle. Gripping it tight in her hand, she stands over Constantine.

For a moment, I think she might end him just as brutally as I always imagined doing myself. But then something changes—her eyes, lined with exhaustion, soften.

"You're not worth it," she says quietly, turning away from him.

Constantine sags in relief even as I grip my sword tight, readying it to finish what I started.

Before I can bring it down against his neck, the mate bond flares once more with pure, radiant power. I watch, both awed and relieved, as it closes in around Constantine. The light that empowered Paige now turns against the monster at our feet, an unstoppable force of retribution.

"Paige?" I call uncertainly.

"Light always claims the darkness," she says. "Energy can't be killed, only remade."

Constantine's breath quickens as he realizes what's happening. "No… no, this isn't how it ends…" he gasps, his voice trembling with terror. He tries to scramble away, but there's nowhere to go, nothing left for him to cling to.

The light tightens, wrapping around him like a vice. His form, already diminished, starts to fracture, his body cracking like porcelain under the pressure. His cries for mercy turn into a gurgling scream, a final, desperate plea that echoes through the smoldering ruins of the library.

Paige doesn't look back, her steps steady as she walks away from him. I follow her, my heart pounding with a mixture of relief and regret. Around us is the evidence of my fire's destruction, but it led to victory, and I have to believe that made it worth it in the end.

I glance behind me as Constantine takes one last, shuddering breath—a sound that cuts off abruptly as the light fully consumes him.

And then, there's silence.

Paige leans against me, exhausted but triumphant.

"It's over," she whispers, her voice filled with both relief and sorrow.

I pull her close, pressing a kiss to her temple. "And your magic?"

"Restored," she says, though the happiness I expect isn't there.

"You're okay?"

"I'm fine," she reassures me. "His destruction has given me back what he took."

Her words are lined with sorrow, but I nod, glad to be done with it. To be alive.

"It's really over then," I say, though the words feel strange in my mouth, as if I'm still trying to convince myself that it's true.

I look out at what has become of the library and can't help but wonder—what will happen to the worlds that were lost? The stories that are now nothing but ash? And what has become of Astronia while we've been gone?

19

PAIGE

At Aries' insistence, I conjure a portal. It shimmers before us, the daylight shining through it a stark contrast to the smoldering, gray ruins of the Athenaeum. But I don't move toward it. Instead, I stare with an aching heart at the destruction surrounding us—the ash and rubble that was once a sanctuary of knowledge and life.

The library is gone, and with it, a part of me has been lost too.

Aries' hand in mine keeps me grounded, his presence a steady anchor. "We need to go, Paige," he says gently. "Our world still needs us."

I can't bring myself to point out that Astronia is not just our world; it's the only one left in all the realms.

Everything else is gone.

Instead, I nod, though the weight of everything we've lost presses heavily on my chest. Our people in Astronia need us now. I won't fail them like I failed the library.

Together, we step through the portal, leaving the ruins of the Athenaeum behind. On the other side, we emerge into a scene of quiet aftermath. The battlefield is still, the sounds of clashing swords and battle cries replaced by the soft murmurs of soldiers tending to the wounded and gathering the fallen. The air is thick with the scent of smoke, but the battle is over.

Constantine's portal monsters have all been destroyed.

Relief washes over me as I see familiar faces—Leo, Blossom, and Mag—standing together near the edge of the field. They're alive, whole.

"Paige," Blossom calls—and then to the others, "Hey guys, they're back!"

Leo strides forward, pulling Aries into a tight hug. "Good to see you in one piece," he says before turning to me. "I think this means I owe you two life debts. Gods, I thought Aries was an over-achiever."

He winks, and I shake my head.

Bingo appears beside me, nudging my hip and earning a scratch behind the ears. I do my best to ignore the blood coating his mouth and staining his massive paws. None of it seems to be his own, at least.

Mag pulls me into a tight hug. When he releases me, he claps Aries on the shoulder and offers a rare, genuine smile. "Glad to see you two back here. You missed all the fun."

The relief on their faces is a balm to my soul, but it's short-lived as the reality of what we've lost crashes over me.

Blossom, ever perceptive, steps closer, her expression growing serious. "Is Constantine…?"

"He's gone," I manage to say, my voice barely above a whisper. "But the Athenaeum… it's… it's gone too. The library, the books… it's all gone. We stopped him in the end, but I couldn't save it."

The smiles fade from their faces, replaced by a mix of shock and sorrow.

Mag's hand falls from Aries' shoulder.

Leo steps closer to me, his expression softening. "Mag

explained your world to me—the library's purpose and what it means to you. I'm so sorry, Paige."

Through the mate bond, Aries' guilt is a weight on his shoulders. He feels terrible, like it's his fault, but it's not.

He was protecting me.

Blossom's eyes widen with concern, and even Mag's usual stoic demeanor cracks as she murmurs, "All those worlds…"

I nod, the grief threatening to overwhelm me again. "It's all gone. All of it. And I couldn't… I couldn't do anything."

Aries wraps an arm around me, pulling me close, his presence a comfort as the reality of what we've lost sinks in. "That's not true," he says softly. "You destroyed Constantine. You saved Astronia."

Before I can respond, a young soldier rushes toward us. He's breathless and without a single speck of blood on him, but his urgency cuts through the somber mood.

"Your Highness," he pants, addressing both Aries and me with a bow. "A messenger arrived from the castle with news—Queen Dorthea has been removed from the throne."

"What?" Aries stiffens, his eyes narrowing as he steps forward. "Who would dare—"

"The council, Your Highness," the soldier interrupts, his voice shaking. "They've declared that they can no longer trust the royal family to protect the kingdom. They've removed Queen Dorthea from the throne and have assumed full control of the land as the governing body."

Aries snarls, and Leo's expression flashes with matching outrage. "Where is my mother now?" Aries demands.

"She's being held in the castle under armed guard. They're claiming it's for her protection, but… she's a prisoner in her own home."

I feel a surge of anger and disbelief. After everything we've fought for, after all the sacrifices, the council dares to overthrow the queen? To imprison her?

Aries turns to me, his expression hard, determined. "We need to go. Now."

Blossom, Leo, and Mag are already moving, their own anger fueling their steps as they prepare to accompany us. The relief of victory is gone, replaced by a renewed sense of urgency. This isn't over—not yet.

But as we make our way toward camp, I can't help but think of the library again. Blossom is right, all those worlds gone, reduced to nothing but memories and ash. The ache in my chest remains, and I pause, glancing back at the charred earth where Constantine's dark portal opened to carry us away.

We defeated him, but in the end, that didn't matter.

In some ways, he still won.

"Paige," Aries says, his voice pulling me back to the present. "Let's go home."

His words are firm but gentle, a reminder that our fight isn't finished. I nod, pushing the grief down as I focus on what needs to be done.

"Let's get your crown back," I say, my voice steady despite the sorrow still lingering in my heart.

IT TAKES US A FEW HOURS OF FLYING TO MAKE THE TRIP HOME. Aries carries me and Blossom while Leo carries Mag and Bingo. Several others accompany us—all winged shifters and some of our best warriors. I tell myself that last part doesn't matter. That we aren't flying to yet another battle. But I can't shake the feeling that's exactly what this will be.

When we land, we drop Blossom, Mag, and the others at the barracks and then make our way to the castle. The corridors inside are oppressively quiet as Aries, Leo, and I make our way toward the suite where Queen Dorthea is being held. We agreed to try diplomacy first, but now that I'm here, I'm not sure that's a strategy I'm capable of carrying out.

The council here in Astronia is beginning to remind me of the one I dealt with back at the Athenaeum. Their betrayal of their king and queen has painted a bull's eye on their heads as far as I'm concerned.

And my magic won't miss once I fire the shot.

Now, Aries walks beside me, his jaw set, eyes forward, while Leo leads the way through the winding halls to the room where our scouts confirmed Dorthea is being held. Mag and Blossom are at the barracks with the soldiers, waiting to hear what orders the council will give the army now that it's home.

The three of us are silent, but the tension is palpable, a storm brewing beneath the surface. I'm barely keeping my emotions in check—the grief over the library's destruction simmering dangerously close to the surface. I need to focus, but it's hard. So hard.

As we turn a corner, we come face to face with Esma and Porthew. Esma's eyes light up with a predatory gleam as she spots Aries while Porthew's expression is cold, calculating. A few guards I don't recognize trail behind them, their stances rigid and unfriendly.

"Well, well," Esma says, her voice dripping with false sweetness. "If it isn't our wayward prince and his entourage. I was wondering when you'd show yourselves."

"You mean you wondered when we would return from the war we fought to save this kingdom while you sat on your asses?" I snap.

Porthew stutters like he can't believe I just said that.

Out of the corner of my eye, I'm pretty sure I see Leo smirking.

Esma's eyes narrow. "Watch how you speak to your country's leadership."

She's not my leader, and those words are on the tip of my

tongue before I realize that, whether I want it or not, Astronia is my country now. It's not like I have anywhere else to go.

The realization renders me silent. Esma smirks like she thinks she's won.

"Let us pass," Aries says, exhaustion lining every word. "We need to clean up. Sleep in a bed. Then we can discuss this."

"I'm afraid we cannot allow that," Porthew says, his tone flat and dismissive. "The council has decided that your residency in the castle is no longer appropriate. You will all need to find accommodations elsewhere, effective immediately."

Aries blinks.

I watch as the words hit him and Leo like a blow. Before either of them can respond, I step forward, anger surging through me, fueled by the grief I've been struggling to contain.

"You don't get to decide that," I snap. "Your bullshit manipulations might have gotten you this far, but this isn't your kingdom to rule."

Esma's gaze shifts to me, her eyes narrowing as if I'm nothing more than a mere nuisance. "Ah, the little mage," she sneers, taking a step closer to Aries.

I zero in on how close she's standing to him and struggle to breathe through the rage. She's baiting me. I know it, but that doesn't mean it isn't working. "I'm surprised you haven't already run back to wherever it is you came from. You must realize there's no place for you here. Not in Astronia, and certainly not beside Aries. He has nothing to offer you, especially now. I, on the other hand, might have something to offer him—"

I close the distance between us, shoving so close that our bodies touch as I say, "If you touch him, I will kill you right here."

Something about my expression must convey that I mean it because she squeaks in response and motions to the guards, who step forward.

Aries. His glare blazes with a heat I feel in my own belly. But instead of lashing out, he holds himself in check.

"We will speak tomorrow," Aries says in a clipped tone. "Once we've all rested."

"Yes," Esma says, getting ahold of herself smoothly. She looks at Aries then Leo and says, "I would enjoy speaking with you both in the morning. There may yet be a compromise for one of you."

The insinuation is clear, and it takes everything in me not to strike out with my magic. All along, Esma has angled for power, and now she thinks she's finally in a position to take what she wants. The thought makes my blood boil.

"You think you can just replace his mother on the throne?" I shoot back, my voice rising. "You think you can steal what's rightfully theirs and the people here will just let you do it? Well, I won't let you. And if you try—"

"Paige," Aries says sharply, his hand gripping my arm, silencing me before I can say more.

But I'm not finished. I shrug off his grip and glare at Esma, my emotions finally spilling over. "You're nothing but a power-hungry—"

"That's enough," Aries cuts in, his voice firm, though I can feel the tension radiating from him. He turns his gaze to Esma, his tone icy. "You don't get to make demands of me, Esma. Nor of Leo or Paige."

Esma's smile tightens, her eyes flashing with frustration. "Perhaps not yet," she says smoothly, but there's an edge to her voice now. "But the council has decreed that you're to leave the castle tonight. The guards will escort you out."

Porthew nods, his expression impassive. "Consider this a courtesy. We don't want to make a scene."

At his words, I notice that the soldiers have their weapons slightly raised and dark scowls fixed on their faces. These are not the same kind and friendly men I fought beside a few days ago.

For the first time, I realize we really have no choice but to leave this place—tonight.

My anger flares again, but Aries tightens his grip on my arm, pulling me back. I know he's right—we can't afford to escalate things here, not when the council holds the upper hand. But it's hard to swallow it down, especially when every fiber of my being is screaming to fight back, to defend what little we have left.

I couldn't save the library, but I can save this land from people like Esma and Porthew.

Aries gives Esma a cold, measured look. "We'll leave tonight," he says, his voice steady. "And meet with you tomorrow as you say. But with a last request."

"You're not exactly in a position to make requests," Porthew says.

"Let us see our mother," Leo puts in. "We will speak with her about our plans so that she can accompany us in the morning when we go."

Esma sighs. Porthew looks as if he wants to refuse, but it's a reasonable request, especially since it's giving them what they want—the Nemos family walking away from their thrones.

Porthew glances at Esma, who nods.

She motions to the soldiers. "Escort them," she says. "And make sure they leave when they're done."

The soldiers finally lower their weapons, obeying Esma's command wordlessly.

Aries glances from Leo back to me, concern flickering in his eyes. "Let's go."

As we continue down the corridor, my thoughts race, trying to piece together a plan, something—anything—that will give us an edge against the council.

When we finally reach Queen Dorthea's room, the guards stationed outside exchange a few words with our armed escorts. Then the door is unlocked, and we're ushered through. Inside, the suite is dimly lit, the heavy curtains drawn, but I'm relieved to see it's not the dungeon and they've at least given her comfortable accommodations.

Behind us, the guards shut the door, sealing us in. At least, we've been granted privacy for the moment.

Queen Dorthea sits by the window, her posture regal despite the circumstances. She turns as we enter, a relieved smile touching her lips.

"My sons," she says, rising to her feet. "And Paige—I'm so glad you're all safe."

Aries crosses the room in a few quick strides, embracing his mother. "I'm sorry we couldn't get to you sooner," he says, his voice thick with emotion. "But we're going to fix this."

Queen Dorthea lets him go, hugging Leo and then me. "I know you will," she says, her voice calm and reassuring. "They can't lock us in our own home."

"Actually, they're kicking us out," Leo tells her, his expression tight. "Effective immediately, we no longer live here. Come morning, we're expected to take you with us and find somewhere else to go."

"They cannot be allowed this coup," Dorthea says, her calm demeanor slipping as the first hints of fury slip through.

"They won't," Leo tells her firmly. He glances at Aries. "Right?"

"Esma is playing a game of her own," he says quietly. "She wants to meet with Leo and me in the morning. I think she plans to offer one of us our crown as long as we agree to make her our queen."

My hands tighten into fists, but I bite back my response. Best to save it for Esma herself. Next time…

"The rest of the council will never go for that," Dorthea says.

"Not outright, no, but I wouldn't put it past her to have some manipulation up her sleeve," Aries says.

"Aries is right," Leo says. "She's been playing all of us from the beginning. We can't underestimate her."

For a moment, no one speaks. I know we're all thinking through possible ways to stop this. But no one offers anything, and the silence stretches until I'm not sure we're going to find a way.

"I could say yes," Leo says softly.

I look up sharply, but he's focused on Aries now.

"I could agree to her terms," Leo goes on. "And once I'm crowned, I can relinquish to you."

Aries shakes his head. "She'll see that coming. Besides, if you relinquish once she's queen, it'll go directly to her—which is what she's hoping for anyway."

"But—"

"If you agree and go through with it, she'll likely have you killed," Aries adds.

Leo scoffs. "She wouldn't dare."

"I think she would," I put in.

"This is bullshit." Leo mutters something to himself and paces near the fireplace. "There has to be another way. Without a dragon on the throne, our lands will suffer."

"Leo's right," Aries says. "The blight may be gone, but without a dragon ruler, the magic blessing Astronia will vanish. The wastelands will spread until there's nothing left."

I want to ask how the council can possibly do this, knowing what kind of destruction it will cause—but I don't bother. Evil has no logic or reason, only hate and hunger. Constantine taught me that.

"You could challenge them to a fight," I remind him. "Win back your seat that way."

But Leo shakes his head. "Now that we've been removed from the throne entirely, a challenge like that has no standing. It won't be recognized or answered."

"Ugh, this is crazy," I fume. "They clearly don't care about what's best for the people. They only want what's best for themselves."

Queen Dorthea sighs, sitting back down with a grace that never falters, even in confinement. "They've always been more concerned with appearances than with the well-being of Astronia."

"They have to be," Leo says with a snort. "If they lose the favor of the people, they lose their seats."

"What do you mean?" I ask.

"The laws my father wrote when he created the council make it clear that, in the absence of a king or queen to dismiss them, the only way a council member can lose their seat is by majority vote of the people."

HIS WORDS HANG IN THE AIR, AND I FEEL SOMETHING CLICK INTO place. My mind races, sifting through everything we've seen, everything we've heard. The council's endless need for validation, their hunger for power, their arrogance. It's all connected, all feeding their belief that they're untouchable.

Aries frowns, catching the shift in my expression. "Paige?"

I look at him, then at Leo, and finally at Queen Dorthea. My heart still aches with the loss of the library, but a new resolve is taking hold, pushing through the grief. "Their egos," I say slowly, the idea solidifying in my mind. "That's what we'll use against them."

"What do you propose?" Dorthea asks.

Quickly, I tell them my idea.

"Is that something you can do?" Aries asks.

"I think so," I say. "I've never tried magic like this, but I don't see why not."

A moment of silence follows as everyone considers the implications. Aries squeezes my hand again, this time with a spark of hope in his eyes.

"Will it be enough?" I ask anxiously.

Aries turns to me, his expression already so much lighter than it was before. "Yes," he says to me, pulling me into his arms. "It's more than enough."

Leo grins, the familiar spark of mischief returning. "Paige, you're a woman after my own heart," he declares. Aries snarls at that, but he laughs. "As a sister," Leo adds pointedly.

I take a deep breath, the weight of the library's loss still there, but for the first time, I can see a way forward. The council may think they've won, but they've underestimated us. They've underestimated what the people of this land are willing to do for this kingdom, for each other.

Diplomacy has its usefulness too.

20

ARIES

Morning arrives gray and quiet. Through the window opposite where I lay, the sun barely pierces through the thick clouds hanging low over Astronia's capital city. Inside the empty barracks room where we slept, the air is damp from the cramped quarters. After leaving my mother's quarters—and several hours of putting our plan into motion—we found a vacant barracks room where Paige and I pushed two single cots together before completely crashing. Leo passed out in a cot shoved against the opposite wall. Bingo, who refused to leave despite the small space, sleeps curled up beside Leo's bed—snoring.

My shoulders are heavy with the weight of the decisions that will be made today. We've traded one battle for another. A war for a war. I ache for the day I can put down my weapons—physical or otherwise.

My mate deserves peace after everything.

But first, we have one more enemy to face.

After waking the others, we all dress quickly. Mag is already coming toward us as we emerge from our room.

"Morning," he says. "I'd ask how you slept, but I'm pretty

sure I already know." He rolls his shoulders, and I know his cot was about the same level of comfort as mine.

Honestly, the ground might have been better.

I grunt an answer, not yet ready for small talk.

Blossom walks up, offering me and the others a mug. "Tea?"

"Bless you," Leo says, taking his quickly as Paige does the same.

"Thanks," Paige says.

I gulp mine without a word, grateful for its bitter warmth.

"Everyone ready then?" Mag asks after a moment.

We all share a look.

"Right then," Mag says. "Paige, Blossom, and I know what to do. But we better get going if we're going to pull this off."

"You remember how to get there?" I ask.

Paige's hand lands on my arm. "I remember," she reassures me. "Go."

I take her face in my hands and kiss her, audience be damned. But for once, no one cracks a single joke at our display. Not even Leo.

I give them all one last look and then hand my empty mug over. Leo does the same. Then we're off, headed to the meeting that will decide all our futures once and for all.

We're met by guards at the castle entrance. They are clearly waiting for us with orders to escort us directly to the throne room. In subdued silence, we make our way through the castle's winding corridors, the familiar paths now feeling foreign, as if the very walls have turned against us. Beside me, Leo's expression is set in a grim line.

If this doesn't work…

Fuck. I can't think about that.

When we reach the throne room, the guards stationed outside don't even meet our eyes as they push open the heavy doors. It's a subtle reminder that the power in this place no longer belongs to us. But that will change.

And these traitors will be the next to go.

Inside, the council has gathered at the far end of the space. The two thrones on the dais sit empty, and I'm glad for it. If Esma or Thorne had decided to lounge in either of them, I might not have managed to control myself long enough for our plan to work.

Instead, a table has been brought in at the base of the steps.

Esma is already seated at the head, a predatory smile curling at the corners of her lips as we enter. Porthew and the other council members are seated around her, their expressions ranging from smug to indifferent.

There's no reason to have this meeting here in this too-large room. Other than rubbing their coup in our faces, of course, which they've cleared deemed a worthy enough cause.

"Good morning, citizens," Esma purrs, her tone dripping with false warmth. "I'm so pleased you could join us. I trust you slept well?"

Thorne snorts at that, but I keep my face impassive as I take a seat across from the flamingo shifter.

"We're here, Esma. Let's get on with it."

Her smile widens, and she leans forward slightly, her eyes gleaming with a mix of anticipation and triumph. "Straight to the point as always, Aries. I do like that about you. Very well." She flicks her gaze to the other council members before settling back on me. "The council has discussed your... unique situation, and we've come to a decision."

"And what might that be?" Leo asks.

Esma's gaze flickers to Leo then back to me. "Our scouts brought word of some changes along our borders."

"What changes are those?" I ask, trying and failing to keep the concern out of my voice.

Esma's expression is tight as she says, "The wastelands have spread farther into Astronia." Her confidence slips for a moment. She glances at Porthew then back to me, raising her chin. "It seems the goddess knows your mother has been removed, and the land is reacting."

The blight.

It had nothing to do with Constantine after all.

Leo curses viciously enough that Esma flinches.

I look out over the faces of the others. None of them meet my eyes. Pathetic.

Esma clears her throat. "It's clear that Astronia needs a dragon shifter on the throne to maintain the land's magic. Without one, the kingdom will suffer—something we all want to avoid." She pauses, letting the words hang in the air for a moment. "However, we also recognize that the crown is a heavy burden, one that perhaps neither of you is fit to carry on your own."

Leo huffs, but I catch his eye, silently telling him to stay calm. We need them to keep talking.

Esma continues, clearly enjoying herself. "The solution is simple. One of you will retain the crown, but only if you agree to marry me and allow the council to govern in your stead. You will be king in name only while the real decisions are made by those of us more... suited to the task."

Leo bristles, but I force myself to remain composed. "So that's your offer? A marriage of convenience, where I or Leo would become nothing more than a figurehead while you and the council rule behind the scenes?"

Esma's smile is cold, her eyes calculating. "Precisely. It's the only way to ensure stability and prosperity for Astronia. And it's a generous offer, considering the circumstances."

"Generous," I repeat, my voice flat. "You mean generous to you and your fellow council members, who stand to gain everything while we lose what the goddess bestowed on us."

Porthew, who has been silent until now, clears his throat. "This is for the good of the kingdom. Surely you understand that."

I lean back in my chair, crossing my arms over my chest. "What I understand is that you've manipulated your way into power, lied to the people, and now you expect us to simply hand over the crown in exchange for... what? A meaningless title?"

"None of this would have been necessary if you'd been willing to cooperate from the start," Porthew snaps, his calm demeanor slipping. "We did what needed to be done."

"Aries kept up his end of the deal," Leo says. "He fought the horde and won by the strength of our army alone. No royal lineage magic. No crown atop his head. And still, you've found a way to steal his birthright."

Thorne glares, but none of them argue Leo's claims.

Good.

"You have lost the confidence of the people," Esma says. "You left them when they needed you most—"

"Liar." I lock eyes with Esma, my gaze unwavering. "Admit it. This is something you'd already begun to plan long before I conveniently went away. This isn't about protecting Astronia—it's about your own greed and ambition. And you know it."

For a moment, the room is silent, the tension so thick it's almost suffocating. Then, Esma's smile returns, but it's more strained now, the cracks beginning to show. "Believe what you want, Aries. But the fact remains that, without the council's leadership, Astronia will fall. The people will suffer. Is that what you want?"

"You're the ones making them suffer," I reply, my voice low but firm. "You've lied to them, manipulated them, all to satisfy your own desire for power. And now you think you can just sweep everything under the rug with a forced marriage and a puppet king?"

Esma's eyes flash with anger. "I wouldn't have had to force you if Aries had just chosen me like he was supposed to the day we met. Porthew assured me he'd grown desperate enough—"

She stops, her face flushing as she realizes what she's just admitted.

The rest of the room is silent, but I note most of the faces of the other council members hold no surprise at her confession of scheming.

Myantha is the only one whose face is pale and eyes are wide as she stares at Esma. "You really set all this in motion," she breathes. Esma doesn't answer. Myantha glances at Porthew then Thorne. "All of you did this and forced me right along with it."

"Don't act like such a saint," Esma snaps at her.

Leo leans forward, his expression stony. "You're admitting that you've taken the crown for yourselves, then. That this was your plan all along—to use us as pawns while you rule in secret."

The council members exchange uneasy glances, but Esma remains defiant. "We've done what was necessary," she repeats, but there's a hint of desperation in her voice now. "The crown belongs to those who can wield it properly, who understand the complexities of ruling a kingdom."

"And who would that be?" I ask, letting the challenge ring clear. "You? The council? Or the people who actually live and breathe Astronia every day?"

Esma scoffs. "The people are imbeciles. They don't understand what it takes to run a kingdom."

Leo shakes his head, a grim smile tugging at his lips. "You really believe that, don't you?"

Esma opens her mouth to respond, but something in the room shifts. The light seems to shimmer around the edges, and I see the flicker of recognition in her eyes a split second before the illusion breaks.

The room, once seemingly empty save for the council and us, is suddenly full of people. Astronians—townspeople, soldiers, nobles—who have been silently watching, listening to every word. Gasps ripple through the crowd as they realize what they've heard, the betrayal laid bare before them.

Esma pales, her eyes widening in horror as she takes in the crowd. The other council members are frozen in shock, their arrogance crumbling in the face of the truth. The people of Astronia have heard everything.

Paige steps forward, the faint glow of her magic still clinging to her as the glamour fades completely. She meets Esma's gaze, and for the first time, I see real fear in Esma's eyes.

"As you said, the people of Astronia are the ones who decide who wears the crown," Paige says, her voice strong, carrying through the room. "And they've heard the truth."

Esma stares at her, speechless, as the murmurs in the crowd grow louder, anger and disbelief mixing into a rising tide. "We can explain," Esma begins.

"Don't bother," a soldier calls out.

"We've heard more than enough," a woman says from somewhere in the back.

"But—" Esma sputters.

"Rule Forty-seven-dash-six of the Agreement," Leo cuts in.

He pushes forward, holding up a copy of the document he's pulled from his jacket.

The room hushes as he reads from it. "If any member of the council, appointed by the king, is found to have committed crimes against the crown, they shall be removed and imprisoned immediately. A trial of their peers will be held to determine a sentence."

Esma squeaks, and her face flushes red. The other council members exchange panicked glances, but it's too late. The illusion has shattered, and with it, their grip on power.

"What about the rest of us?" Myantha calls.

Thorne and Porthew cast me wary looks, but I ignore them. "The law states you must have the favor of the people if not the crown," I say, my voice cutting through the noise. "They trusted you, and you betrayed them. But now, the truth is out. And the people will decide who their true leaders are."

Myantha's shoulders droop, but she doesn't argue.

The crowd erupts, voices calling for justice, for accountability.

I watch as Esma's composure cracks completely, her facade of control crumbling. Without another word, Paige walks calmly over to where the crown rests on the table—a symbol of everything the council tried to steal. She picks it up, the golden metal gleaming in the light, and the room falls into a hushed silence as she turns toward Queen Dorthea.

My mother, who has been watching silently along with the rest of the crowd, steps forward, her gaze steady and full of quiet strength. Paige meets her eyes. Then, with deliberate care, she places the crown back on Dorthea's head, restoring her to her rightful place.

Esma's shock snaps into fury. "No!" she shrieks, her voice high and desperate. "Guards, arrest her! Arrest them all!"

But the guards, the same ones who had followed the council's orders without question, now stand still. Their eyes flicker to Queen Dorthea, to me, and finally to Paige, and it's clear they no longer recognize Esma's authority.

Paige turns slowly, her gaze sweeping over the soldiers who remain unmoving. "No," she says firmly, her voice ringing with command. "Arrest them."

For a moment, no one moves. The tension is so thick it feels like the entire room is holding its breath. Then, as if released from a spell, the guards step forward, shifting their attention from us to the council members. Esma's face twists in panic as the soldiers move toward her and the others.

"You can't do this!" she cries, backing away as the guards close in. "This isn't how it's supposed to be!"

No one speaks up on her behalf.

As the guards lead the council members away, Esma's

shrieks of protest fade into the background. My gaze meets Paige's, and I find a fierce, triumphant light in her eyes that mirrors my own feelings.

The kingdom is safe. The people are safe. And we're finally free of the shadows that have hung over us for so long.

But as the noise of the departing guards and murmuring crowd begins to subside, another feeling rises in my chest—something warmer, more hopeful. My mother catches my eye and inclines her head pointedly toward my mate. I take a step toward Paige, my heart pounding, not with the adrenaline of battle but with the clarity of what I need to do next.

"Paige," I begin, my voice low, just for her despite the crowded room. She turns to me fully, the fierce light in her eyes softening as she reads the emotion in my face.

"Yes?" she asks, her voice a blend of curiosity and something else—something that makes me believe she already knows what I'm about to say.

I reach out, taking both of her hands in mine. The room, the crowd, the entire kingdom seems to fade away, leaving just the two of us in this moment. "We've been through so much together," I say, my voice thick with emotion. "You've stood by me, fought beside me, and shown me what it means to truly love and protect this kingdom."

Her eyes glisten with unshed tears, but she doesn't look away. I can see the understanding there, the connection that has grown stronger with every challenge we've faced.

"I can't imagine ruling Astronia without you," I continue, my grip on her hands tightening just slightly. "I can't imagine my life without you."

She inhales sharply, and I see the tears welling up, though she tries to blink them away. I step closer, our foreheads almost touching, the space between us charged with everything we haven't yet said.

"Paige," I say, my voice barely a whisper now, "will you

marry me and build a life together here with me in Astronia—as its queen?"

For a moment, she doesn't respond—doesn't seem to breathe. But then, a tear slips free, and she nods, a smile breaking through the emotion on her face. "Yes," she whispers, her voice full of joy and relief. "Yes, Aries, I will."

The world rushes back in as I pull her into a tight embrace, the cheers of the crowd swelling around us, but all I can focus on is her—Paige, my mate, my love, my future queen. When I pull back to look at her, the tears in her eyes are mirrored in my own, but for once, there's no sadness here—only the promise of what's to come.

As the crowd continues to cheer, I lean in and press a kiss to her forehead then to her lips, sealing the promise we've just made to each other. This is our new beginning, the start of a life together that we've both fought so hard to build.

And as we turn to face the people of Astronia, hand in hand, I know that, no matter what challenges lie ahead, we will face them together. Astronia will have a mated dragon pair on its throne once again.

21

PAIGE

The grand hall of the castle is a riot of color and light, filled with the hum of voices and the rustle of fine fabrics as Astronia's nobility and citizens gather for the ceremony. Banners in deep blues and golds hang from the high ceilings, catching the sunlight streaming through the stained-glass windows. It feels like the entire kingdom has packed into this space, and for the first time in weeks, the air is thick with hope rather than tension and fear.

I stand up front on the dais beside Aries, my hand in his. The warmth of his skin against mine is a quiet comfort, grounding me in this moment, even as my heart swells with so many conflicting emotions. There's a part of me that still aches with the loss of the Athenaeum, a hollow feeling that hasn't left me since the flames took it. But here, surrounded by the people we fought so hard to protect, that ache is softened by the knowledge that we did it—we saved Astronia.

And now, we're about to see the final piece of that victory fall into place.

Sadness threatens to close in, but I shove it aside. There will be time for mourning the library later. Today, I am determined to celebrate. My eyes catch on the emerald thrones, the inlaid gems glistening where they catch the light. They are equal in shape and size. Partners in every way that matters. Exactly like Aries and me.

My joy flares bright as Queen Dorthea steps forward, her regal presence commanding the room. Even after everything she's been through, she's the epitome of grace and strength. The crowd hushes as she reaches the throne, the murmurs dying down until the only sound is the soft rustle of her gown as she turns to face us all.

"People of Astronia," Dorthea begins, her voice clear and strong, carrying across the hall. "Today, we restore what was lost. Today, we return to the path of truth, justice, and unity. I stand before you, not as a queen who clings to power but as a servant of this kingdom—one who believes in its bright future."

The crowd is silent, every eye fixed on her.

Over Aries' shoulder, I catch Mag's eye. He's dressed in the finest suit I've ever seen. When he sees me watching, he shoots me a huge wink that has me grinning. Next to him, the gnomes stand proudly, their chests puffed up in their tiny little suits and matching hats. I wave at them, and they jump up and down in excitement.

"By the will of the people, and with the guidance of those who have stood by me, I reclaim my rightful place as your queen," Dorthea continues. "But as we look to the future, it is clear that a new chapter must begin. A chapter where the strength of our past meets the promise of tomorrow."

She turns to Aries, and I feel his grip on my hand tighten. He takes a deep breath and steps forward, his eyes never leaving his mother's. Dorthea smiles, a soft, proud smile that makes my heart ache with its quiet emotion.

"In this new chapter, we need a leader who embodies the best of Astronia's spirit," Dorthea says, her voice thick with emotion. "And that leader is my son, Aries."

The crowd erupts into cheers, the sound a wave of approval and hope. I can't help but smile as I watch Aries bow his head, his expression a mixture of humility and determination. He's ready for this—the culmination of everything we've fought for.

Dorthea lifts the crown from her head, the golden metal catching the light as she holds it high. The room falls silent again as she places the crown on Aries' head, the symbol of his new role as king. The weight of it is more than just physical, and I can see the resolve in his eyes as he accepts it.

"I present to you your dragon king," Dorthea announces, her voice steady despite the tears glistening in her eyes. "King Aries of Astronia."

The cheers are deafening, filling the hall with a palpable sense of joy and relief. Behind me, Blossom is the loudest of all, whistling hard enough to make my ears ring. Aries turns to face the crowd, and I can see the pride in his stance, the way he carries himself. He's no longer just a prince fighting for his people—he's their king.

Aries raises a hand, and the crowd quiets again. "Thank you," he says, his voice firm but gentle. "Thank you for your trust, your courage, and your belief in a future where Astronia can thrive. I vow to lead with honor, to protect this land and its people, and to build a kingdom where justice and peace prevail."

As he speaks, I feel a swell of emotion in my chest. This is the man I've fought beside, the man I've come to love with a depth I didn't know I was capable of. And now, we're about to take another step forward—one that will change both of our lives forever.

Aries turns to me, and there's a softness in his eyes that makes my heart skip a beat. He steps closer, and the world narrows to just the two of us, the noise of the crowd fading into the background.

"Paige Murphy, daughter of Hoc Novensile, mate of my soul," he begins, his voice low but steady, full of emotion. "I've walked through fire with you, faced the darkest of days, and found strength in your love. You are my heart, my anchor, and the only one I want by my side—for today and every day to come. Will you be my queen, my partner, my wife?"

My breath catches, tears welling in my eyes as I look into his, seeing the depth of his love and commitment. The moment is charged with everything we've been through, everything we've become together.

I take his hands in mine, holding them tightly as I reply, my voice filled with emotion. "Aries, you are my strength, my courage, my love. I will stand by you, fight with you, and build our future together. Yes, I will be your queen, your partner, your wife—today and always."

"And I am yours—today and always," he murmurs.

The words hang between us, a vow, a promise.

The crowd erupts into cheers once more, and I barely register the sound as Aries pulls me in for a passionate kiss. This moment, this connection—it's everything I could have ever hoped for.

But unlike a normal wedding, it's not over yet.

Dorthea steps up again with another crown in her hands. This one is more delicate than the first, the lines more intricate and set with sapphires and moonstone.

It's the most beautiful thing I've ever seen. I'm so caught up in admiring it that I forget it's meant for me until Dorthea's eyes find mine.

"Paige Nemos, wife of Astronia's dragon king, this crown belongs to you now—a symbol of your rightful place among our people. Do you vow to lead as queen with honor, to protect this land and its people from all enemies, and to build a kingdom where justice and peace prevail?"

"I do," I say, my voice wobbling only slightly.

Dorthea smiles radiantly as she places the crown on my head. She leans down and kisses my cheek lightly then nudges me until I've spun around to face the crowd. Beside me, Aries has done the same.

I grip his hand tight as we both look out over the people.

Behind me, Dorthea calls out, "I present to you, the queen and king of Astronia! Let the celebration begin!"

22

ARIES

The grand hall is alive with laughter, music, and the clinking of goblets as everyone toasts to the future of Astronia. The tension of the past few days has lifted, replaced by the warmth of celebration and the joy of the moment. Everywhere I look, there are smiles—faces filled with hope for the days to come. It's a sight I never thought I'd see again, and it fills me with a sense of contentment I haven't felt in a long time.

Paige is by my side, her hand in mine, as we move through the throng of well-wishers. I steal glances at her when I can, admiring the sight of her in that dress, the crown. The sadness lingers at the edges of her smiles, and I vow to myself to do whatever it takes to help her heal that grief in time.

We're stopped by Blossom whose dress is a radiant blue—a cloudless sky. "Congrats to the happy couple. Have you seen the gnomes?" she asks, a twinkle of amusement in her eyes.

I glance around, not seeing them anywhere. "Not since the ceremony," I admit. "Why?"

Blossom tilts her head toward the far corner of the room

where a cluster of guests is gathered around a small table. "Because they've apparently found the dessert table—and I don't think there are any cupcakes left."

I follow her gaze and spot Kitty perched on top of the table, her raccoon face smeared with icing and a wide grin splitting her face. Kitty's black bow tie is a nice touch, especially with white icing staining one corner. The gnomes stand around her, their hands covered in chocolate, looking thoroughly pleased with themselves.

"They ate all of them?" Paige asks, half-laughing, half-exasperated.

"Every last one," Blossom confirms with a playful snort. "I should've known better than to let them near the desserts."

"Maybe, but look how happy they are," I say, chuckling as I watch the gnomes bicker over the last remaining crumbs.

Kitty catches sight of us watching and ducks her head, slinking away quickly. "Best wedding ever!" Ned declares, icing dripping down his arm.

"Clearly," Paige says, shaking her head in mock disapproval. "I suppose we should have expected this."

"We'll need to order more sweets before there's a revolt," I joke, squeezing her hand gently.

As we move away from the dessert table, Mag joins us, a cup of ale in his hand. "Decent party, Your Highness." He winks at Paige. "How does it feel to be ruler of the free world?"

Bingo appears then, pressing his large body into Paige's side.

"It feels like a dream," Paige replies, but there's a note of sadness in her voice that I can't ignore. "But I can't help feeling like something's missing."

We all fall quiet, the weight of what's been lost hanging between us. The destruction of the Athenaeum is a shadow that none of us can shake, even in the midst of this celebration.

"I am sorry for what happened to the Athenaeum," I say

quietly, breaking the silence. "It wasn't just a place; it was a part of who you are. I never meant to take that away."

"You didn't," Paige says firmly. Her constant reassurance that she doesn't blame me has been the only thing keeping me from fully giving in to the guilt. "You were protecting me. If you hadn't… I can't even think about it."

"Paige is right," Blossom says. "None of it is your fault. Still…" Her gaze is distant. "So many stories... so much knowledge... gone. It's hard to accept."

Mag nods. "I know it started out as a prison sentence, but…" He glances at Blossom. "It was also the place that brought us together."

Paige's hand tightens around mine, her fingers cool against my skin.

Blossom sighs softly. "Maybe we should see it one last time. What's left of it, I mean. Before we move on."

Mag looks up, his expression thoughtful. "You know, that might be what we all need—to say goodbye properly."

Paige turns to me, her eyes searching mine, and I can see the unspoken question there. I nod, understanding exactly what she's feeling. "Yes," I agree. "One last goodbye before starting our new life."

Blossom perks up, her sadness tempered by determination. "Then let's go," she says, her voice firm. "We owe it to ourselves, to the Athenaeum, to see it one more time."

"Now?" I ask, glancing around.

Blossom shrugs. "Why not? Everyone's drunk anyway. No one's going to miss us this late in the party."

She's not wrong. The hour has grown late already. So late that any absence on my part will be seen as me stealing away with my new bride. "All right," I say. "Let's do it."

Paige smiles at her, a bittersweet expression that echoes my own feelings. "Thank you," she says quietly. "For understanding."

I draw her hand to my lips and kiss it. "It's the least I can do for my queen."

We end up in the gardens where Paige conjures a portal that shimmers darkly beneath the moonlight. Bingo trots up behind us as we enter, followed by the gnomes and Kitty, who seem to be running from something—or someone. I don't bother to ask who as we usher them through the portal along with us. Just before the portal winks closed, another figure slips in.

"Leo." I blink at the sight of my brother here in this place.

"You were really going to leave me behind again," he accuses.

"We aren't staying," I tell him.

"Is that what you thought the first time you—whoa. What the hell happened here?" He stares at the ashen walls surrounding us.

"A fire," I say quietly.

He looks at me sharply. "Your fire?"

The others have fanned out, wandering among the debris still smoldering.

"Yes," I say.

"How? I mean, it looks like it just happened. But it's been days since…"

"Time works differently here," I explain. "It's probably only been minutes or hours since everything burned."

Leo opens his mouth, undoubtedly to fire off more questions but Ned's voice interrupts.

"What did you do to it?" he suddenly wails. "Everything is gone."

Paige winces, and we share a look. In the chaos of the orc war, we never told the gnomes everything that happened here.

I step forward. "I did it," I tell them.

"You cooked it," Ned accuses.

"With your dragon fire," Zed adds.

"Yes," I answer.

"Why would you do that?" Ned demands, marching up to me with a glare.

I kneel so that we're a bit closer to eye level. "Because Constantine was going to kill Paige if I didn't."

Ned stops, frowning. The anger goes out of his eyes, and he says, "In that case, thank you for stepping in. Paige always thinks she can save herself, but we've been doing it this whole time."

"And it's exhausting," Zed says solemnly, icing covering the lower half of his face.

Behind me, Paige snorts.

I bite back a smile, nodding as seriously as I can. "Now, she has me, so you don't have to worry."

"Well, that's a relief," Zed says. "We would much rather eat cookies all day and let Kitty chase mice in the stables."

"You like it in Astronia then?" I ask.

"We love it," Ted chimes in, all of them nodding happily. "We live like kings!" he adds then ducks his head sheepishly. "No offense."

"None taken."

"Hey, what is this?" Blossom asks from across the space.

Paige and I join her along with Mag and the others. She gestures to something lying among the debris and ashes.

An ancient-looking tome, its edges burnt and flaking. But the cover itself and the faded lettering, though tattered, is readable enough.

"Book of Origins," Blossom reads. She glances up at Paige. "I've never seen this book before. Have you?"

"No," Paige says, brows crinkling in confusion.

The others join us, Mag and the gnomes each taking turns examining the book, but no one remembers it.

A vague memory surfaccs. I frown, turning to Paige. "When we went into the heart of the library, there was a book on display in the center of the room. Constantine attacked before I could see it clearly, but this looks a lot like what I glimpsed."

"Strange that it would survive when nothing else did," Blossom says. She reaches for the cover, pulling it open to a cloud of ash and dust that swirls into the air.

She leans back, coughing as we all fan the dust away. But then, something unexpected happens. The ashes don't just dissipate—they begin to shimmer, catching the faint light like tiny stars, and then they start to swirl, gathering into a vortex above the book.

"Uh…is it supposed to do that?" Leo asks, taking a step back.

"Should we be worried?" Blossom puts in.

Fear twists my gut as I brace myself for Constantine reborn —or some other monster. But Paige replies, her voice tinged with wonder. "I don't think so. Look."

The swirling ash coalesces, the glowing particles forming into the shape of a figure—a tall, ethereal woman, her body composed of shimmering light and glittering dust. Her eyes are deep pools of knowledge, her hair flowing like pages in a breeze, and when she smiles, it's as if all the wisdom of the universe is reflected in her gaze.

Even so, her skin is charred in several places, and her expression is lined with exhaustion.

"Athenaeum…" Paige breathes, staring up at the apparition, at the same time Leo and I both whisper, "Goddess."

We all exchange a startled look.

The figure before us nods, her voice echoing with a melodic resonance. "I am Athenaeum, the spirit of the library, the guardian of all stories. Though the physical structure has been lost, I remain." She coughs, and I wonder for how much longer. "I am known by many names. And many worlds."

"You're the goddess from Astronian legends," I say. "The creator of our world. I've seen you in our history books."

"How?" Paige asks.

"Energy cannot be killed, only remade," the goddess says with a secret smile. "Speaking of which, it seems Astronia has fallen into good hands once again. Well done, both of you. And you," she says to Leo whose eyes widen at the compliment.

"So, wait, if you're here… does that mean the library is still…alive?" Mag asks.

"In a manner of speaking, yes," the goddess replies. "The books may be gone, but the stories live on within me. They are eternal as long as there are those who remember and seek to preserve them."

"How?" he asks. "This place was scorched."

I wince, but the Athanaeum is unfazed. "As I said, energy cannot be destroyed, young Keeper, only transmuted."

"So, the worlds contained inside the stories…" Paige asks tentatively.

Athenaeum offers her a reassuring smile. "They survived."

"Well, that's a relief," Blossom says. "But what about the monsters we stopped from escaping for so many years? Without the library to contain them…?"

The spirit's expression grows somber. "The balance has indeed shifted. The Athenaeum was not only a sanctuary for stories but also a ward against the darkness. Without it, those barriers have weakened. The creatures once held at bay are now free."

"When you say free…" I begin warily. "Where exactly did they go?"

"Some are set free inside their own worlds. Some found a way out into another realm entirely. Some escaped into Astronia before you stopped them."

"What happens to the worlds now?"

"It's hard to say without a central hub to act as a stopgap." True concern flits over her pale features. "If left unchecked, the core of the universe will react to the imbalance… and I'm honestly not sure what that will look like. Most likely, the worlds will rip apart, and the universe will experience a reset."

"All that from the creatures in these stories being loosed?" I ask.

She eyes me, nodding grimly. "The worlds were never meant to overlap." Her expression turns thoughtful. "Except where Fate has intervened."

She's talking about Paige and me finding one another. Mag and Blossom too. And while Fate has my gratitude for it, I can't overlook the danger that awaits us now. Dread roils inside me as I contemplate more battles to be fought.

It never fucking ends.

Paige steps forward, determination hardening her features. "Is there anything we can do? We can't just leave things like this."

The spirit's gaze turns to Paige, her eyes softening with something like affection. "Your magic, Paige, has always been the key. You hold within you the power to create and restore, to bring balance where there is chaos. You have already done so much more than you realize."

Paige looks puzzled. "What do you mean?"

The spirit smiles, a knowing, almost cryptic expression. She opens her mouth to respond, but her form flickers, and the words are lost as she blinks in and out.

"Whoa, you're breaking up or something," Mag says.

"What did she say?" Paige asks.

Athenaeum flickers back into sight. Her words come through, but there's a buzzing behind them now. "You will understand in time. Trust in yourself, in your magic. The Athenaeum may be gone, but its essence endures in you."

"Me?" Paige echoes. "What do you mean?"

"Why do you think I chose you?"

"I don't know—"

Before Paige can ask more, the spirit begins to fade, the light dimming as she speaks her final words. "The stories never truly end, Paige. They evolve, just as you must. This is not the end but a new beginning."

And with that, the spirit of the Atheneum vanishes along with the Book of Origins she came from, leaving us standing in the ruins, surrounded by the quiet echoes of what once was.

23

PAIGE

The air is thick with smoke and silence as I stand in the center of what was once a grand library and—more than that, a home. Now, nothing more than a cavern of ashes and debris remains. The Athanaeum's cryptic parting words press down on me. *This is not the end but a new beginning*.

The way she'd looked right at me made my magic tingle.

As if she'd been speaking more to it than me.

Maybe she had been. Maybe…

My heart races, a mix of hope and fear swirling in my chest as I look around. I know what I have to do, but I have no idea if I can actually pull it off.

"What are you thinking, Paige?" Aries asks, his voice soft but laced with concern. His hand rests on my shoulder, grounding me as I stare at the ashen ruins.

"I'm thinking…" I begin then hesitate, swallowing hard as I try to gather my thoughts. "I'm thinking I have to try something. But I don't know if it'll work."

Blossom steps closer, her gaze steady. "You heard what the

Athenaeum said. Your magic is the key. If anyone can do this, it's you."

"I know, but…" I trail off, my eyes scanning the destruction around us. "What if I can't? What if I try and nothing happens? What if I make things worse?"

Mag chimes in, his usual cheerfulness subdued. "If she's telling the truth, the end of the world is coming. It can't get worse than that."

Blossom shoves him lightly and rolls her eyes. "Not helpful."

"I think the last few months have shown us it can always get worse," I say dryly.

"You can't think like that," Aries adds, his voice firm. "You've done the impossible before. You can do it again."

I look into his eyes, seeing the belief there, the trust he has in me. It's enough to make me take a deep breath, even though doubt still lingers in the back of my mind.

"Okay," I say, more to myself than to anyone else. "Here we go."

The others step back, giving me space as I close my eyes and reach deep inside myself, searching for the well of magic that's always there, pulsing just beneath the surface. I can feel it, a warm, vibrant energy that thrums in time with my heartbeat.

Wrapping my hands around the magic, I imagine the Athenaeum as it was—the rows and rows of books, the tall, towering shelves, the quiet hum of ancient knowledge that filled the air.

I take a deep breath, and as I exhale, I let the magic flow out of me. It starts as a gentle pulse, but I push harder, feeling the energy surge through me, gathering in my fingertips. My eyes open as the air around me begins to shimmer, the ground beneath my feet vibrating with the power I'm channeling.

It's not enough yet.

"Come on," I whisper, focusing on the image in my mind. "Come on, work."

The ashes on the ground stir, lifting into the air in swirling tendrils of dust. The debris shifts, drawn together as the magic takes hold, the ruins around me beginning to reform. I can feel the strain, the effort it takes to hold the image steady in my mind, to keep the magic flowing without faltering.

I hear a gasp behind me, but I don't turn. Not yet. The magic is building, the pressure inside me mounting as I pour everything I have into this one act of creation.

This is so much more than anything I've done before.

I draw on a deeper well—of magic and memory and emotion. I draw on everything I am. Every experience this place ever gave me.

Late-night patrols and early morning cataloging. Reshelving with Hoc. Laughing with Blossom. Flirting with Mag. Chasing the gnomes and bribing them with candy. Bingo's unfaltering loyalty. Kitty's mischievous purr.

I don't just think about restoring the static, lifeless items this time. I remember the essence that made this place what it was. What it could be again. Besides, nothing here was ever static. Even the books had heartbeats.

I concentrate on the way they pulsed. The way they breathed.

Energy cannot be destroyed, only remade. Transmuted.

Unlike the times before this, today I don't try to recreate a dead thing. I transmute what's still here. What's always been here.

Pulsing. Beating. Breathing.

I open my eyes and see the dust and ash swirl faster, coalescing into solid forms—shelves, walls, stacks of books. I can feel the library taking shape around me, piece by piece, but it's like holding a delicate thread that could snap at any moment.

"Paige…" Aries's voice is tight, filled with worry.

"Not yet," I murmur, my voice trembling with the effort. "Almost there…"

Sweat coats my brow, but I don't stop.

The shelves rise, row upon row, just as I remember them. The Sea Creatures section to the left with the tall, glass-fronted cases. The Winged Creatures section to the right, the shelves filled with volumes on dragons, gryphons, and other creatures of the sky.

The central staircase begins to form, spiraling upward to the upper levels where the restricted section lies. Behind me, I picture Hoc's office, the cluttered desk, the shelves overflowing with scrolls and ancient manuscripts. Grief pangs inside me, and I pour it—along with my love for him—into the stream of creation.

I can feel my strength waning, the magic starting to slip through my grasp.

"Almost there," I whisper, gritting my teeth as I push harder, forcing the last remnants of my magic into the spell.

The elevator appears, and as it slides into place, I feel the library solidify around me, the magic settling, the tension in the air dissipating.

Exhaustion slams into me, and my eyes slide shut as my knees give out.

Aries catches me before I can hit the floor.

"Whoa, easy," he says against my ear.

"Is she okay?" Blossom asks.

I suck in a deep, steadying breath. "I'm fine. Just tired."

"Paige, look," Ned exclaims.

Slowly, I open my eyes, and what I see takes my breath away. The Athenaeum stands before me, just as it was, every detail perfect, down to the soft glow of the magical lamps that light the space.

I inhale, and the familiar scent of crisp pages and printed paper greets me.

It's a time capsule restored to perfection.

"You did it," Blossom breathes, her voice filled with awe.

I turn to them, tears welling in my eyes, and for a moment, I can't speak. The relief, the joy, the sheer disbelief that I actually managed to do it overwhelms me.

Finally, I find my voice, though it's choked with emotion. "Welcome home," I whisper, my tears spilling over as I smile at them. "Welcome home."

The others look around, taking in the sight of the restored library, their faces lit with wonder. Aries pulls me into his arms, holding me close as I finally let the tears fall. It's done. The Atheneum lives again.

"Um, guys." Blossom's voice is barely louder than a whisper, but there's a note of urgency that blares like an alarm.

She holds up her arm, and all of my joy turns to dread as I spot the familiar tattoo inking itself onto her skin. My stomach twists as I look over and see the same design etching itself into Mag's arm.

"Does this mean we're prisoners again?" Blossom asks quietly.

"I…" I nearly choke on the words, horror spreading slowly through me as I realize my big save might have just cost them their freedom—again.

I force myself to look down at my own arm, and sure enough, my head librarian tattoo is back. A familiar bond follows quickly after—my connection to the library's soul. Returned to me once again.

"Paige's magic recreated things to exactly how they were before," Mag says, his words twisting with pain. "So, I guess that means the tattoos and the prison sentence."

Fuck.

What have I done?

"Uh, guys. Not exactly how they were," Ned pipes up. "Look."

We all turn to where Ned is pointing, and my breath catches. In the far corner of the library, a faint, pulsating glow catches our attention. It's not a threatening light—at least, it doesn't feel that way—but it's definitely something new. Something that wasn't here before.

"What is that?" Mag asks, his voice barely above a whisper.

Aries keeps a protective arm around my waist as we cautiously move closer to the light. The others follow, their steps tentative, as if they're all as wary as I am about what we'll find.

As we approach, the glow becomes more defined, revealing a small, ornate pedestal that wasn't part of the original library. Atop it rests a single pristine book, its cover made of something that looks almost like glass, with light swirling just beneath the surface. The title is etched in shimmering letters: *The Book of Beginnings.*

"What the hell…?" Aries murmurs, his brow furrowing as he studies the book.

"I don't remember this," I say, my voice trembling. "This wasn't here before."

Blossom inches closer, her eyes wide with a mix of curiosity and fear. "It's…beautiful," she whispers, reaching out but hesitating just before her fingers nearly touch the cover. "But what does it mean?"

My mind races, trying to piece together what this could signify. The Athenaeum's spirit had said this was a new beginning. Could this book be part of that? Is it something I created without realizing it, or was it something the library itself—alive with stories and magic—brought into existence?

"I'm not sure," I admit, my voice barely audible. "But I think this might be part of what the Athenaeum meant. A new beginning…a way forward, maybe?"

"But what does it do?" Mag asks, his gaze locked on the book as if it might suddenly spring to life.

I can't blame him. After everything Constantine did—using these books against us—I think it'll be a long while before any of us open a book without first considering the consequences.

But… this one feels different.

It feels like the opposite of the threats we've come to fear.

With its shining crystal cover, translucent and inviting as if it has nothing to hide, this book feels like hope.

"Maybe it's meant to be our fresh start," I say slowly, the realization dawning on me. "To rewrite how the library works. To make the future whatever we want."

A silence falls over the group as everyone contemplates the possibilities. I reach out and place my hands gently against the cover. The Book of Beginnings pulses beneath my touch as if waiting for us to decide what comes next.

Tentatively, I open the cover.

The first page is blank.

I turn it over and find the next page blank too. And the next. And the next.

Magic ripples, and a black pen appears on the platform next to the book. I snatch my hand away.

Blossom snorts. "Subtle."

I look from the pen to the blank page, and I realize, unlike the others, this book isn't telling us a story. We're writing it. In real time, moment by moment.

I pick up the pen and press it to the page, starting from the beginning: *This is the story of the Athanaeum, a magical library, a protector and keeper of worlds. Here, everyone who serves is free and does so by choice.*

Once the words are formed, magic winks from every corner of the space. The lights flare and then return to normal. The bond inside me sighs as if in relief.

Mag and Blossom look up at me sharply.

"My tattoo is gone," Blossom breathes.

"So is mine," Mag says, his voice thick with emotion.

They share a look and then face me again. My eyes fill with tears of gratitude and relief.

"So, what happens now?" Mag asks, breaking the quiet. "Are you going to take up the mantle again, Paige?"

I hesitate, the weight of the question settling over me. The Athenaeum was a huge part of my life, but so much has changed. The thought of being its Head Librarian again feels… wrong, like I'm trying to step back into a role that no longer fits.

A role that never really fit at all, if I'm being honest.

Besides, I've already sworn a vow to another world.

"I'm not sure I'm meant to lead anymore," I admit, my voice soft. "My journey took me somewhere new. And I think that's what this book is about. We get to choose now. Like we didn't get a choice before." Blossom and Mag both nod. "But if not me…then who?"

The words hang in the air, heavy with uncertainty, until Blossom steps forward, her expression determined. "I'll do it," she says, surprising everyone. "But only if Mag will do it with me."

Mag blinks, taken aback. "You want me to help run the library? With you?"

Blossom shrugs. "You know these stories' tricks better than anyone. And we've always worked well together, haven't we?"

He smirks, but it vanishes quickly as he studies her. "Are you sure you want to be here, though? After being trapped here for so long…"

"I want a place I belong," she says quietly. "A home. A place I can have roots."

"Roots, huh?" Mag asks, warming to the idea if his expression is any indication. He steps closer to her, clearly uncaring that they have a full audience. "Does this have anything to do with finally claiming me as your mate?"

Blossom's jaw drops. "You knew?"

Mag laughs. "Of course I knew. You're a terrible liar."

"Why didn't you say anything?" she demands.

"Why didn't you?"

She looks like she might take a swing at him, so I wince as

he swoops in and kisses her instead. But she surprises me by throwing her arms around him and kissing him back.

The gnomes cheer.

Bingo growls, and Kitty hisses.

I laugh, silenced only when Aries takes the opportunity to lean in and kiss me too. There's joy reflected in his gaze, but there's also relief. I know exactly how he feels.

Walking away from the library, leaving it in such capable hands, feels right.

But I pull away just as Mag does the same.

"Is that a yes?" he asks Blossom.

"I'm the one that asked you," she fires back.

"In that case, hell yeah," Mag says. "I'll run the library with you. Mate."

Blossom softens, her eyes shining bright. She looks over at me and says, "I guess you're out of a job."

I laugh. "I'm only transferring to another kind of public service."

Aries winks, and I quickly scrawl Blossom and Mag's names into the book as Head Librarians—together. Magic ripples, and then fresh words appear on the page. "It says to place your palms on the page," I tell them.

Blossom and Mag step forward, each of them pressing their palms to where I scrawled their names as head librarians. The moment their skin touches the parchment, light flares, and a surge of magic sweeps through the room, swirling around them like a gust of wind.

Like water being emptied from a cup, I feel my bond with the library drain away. Blossom and Mag both gasp, and I know that bond has transferred to them, the magic forming a connection that's as strong as the one I once had. As the light fades, Blossom and Mag pull their hands back, their eyes wide with awe.

New markings line their arms.

"I can feel it," Blossom breathes, her voice filled with wonder. "It's like the library is a part of me now."

"Same here," Mag adds, flexing his fingers as if testing the new power coursing through him. "Incredible."

I glance down at my arm, noticing that the familiar tattoo—the mark of my bond with the library—has vanished, leaving my skin clear. The Athenaeum has chosen its new guardians, and it's time for me to let go.

My heart pangs as I think of Hoc, but I also know he would want this for me—and for them. Before I can dwell on that thought, the gnomes shuffle forward, looking nervous.

"Uh, Paige?" Ned begins, his voice hesitant. "Do we have to stay here? Or…can we choose where we want to go?"

I smile down at them, affection swelling in my chest. "You can choose, of course. You've all earned that right."

The gnomes exchange glances, and then Zed steps forward, clearing his throat. "We choose Astronia. We like it there. The queen fusses over us, and we get lots of treats except—"

"Except," I prompt.

They exchange another glance, and I swear they have a silent conversation with one another. Then, Ned turns back to me and says, "Well, maybe we could visit here once in a while for candy… and, you know, to visit Blossom and Mag."

I grin. "Of course."

"Don't forget pizza," Blossom adds.

Kitty meows in agreement, swiping a paw playfully at Mag's leg. The gnomes cheer, their excitement palpable.

Everyone laughs at that.

Then Leo speaks up. He's been quiet, taking it all in, but now he looks at Bingo, who's been quietly watching the exchange. "What about you, Bingo? Where do you want to go?" he asks.

Bingo opens his mouth, but the only sound that comes out is a whine. I frown, noting that the hellhound looks even more grumpy and out of sorts than usual.

"Bingo, are you okay?" I ask.

Bingo snarls, but the sound is abruptly cut off as a sudden swirl of magic envelops the hound. The light grows brighter, spinning faster until it's almost blinding. When it finally fades, we all gasp in shock.

Standing where Bingo had been moments before is a beautiful woman. She's young, probably not any older than me, but her sparkling blue eyes contain depths of pain and a past that suggest she's far older than her appearance conveys. Her blonde hair falls in waves down her back, swishing as she angles her body to glance down at herself in awe.

"What…?" I stammer, trying to process what I'm seeing.

She looks up and meets my eyes. "Paige."

There's a trace of an accent in her tone and her voice, though rich and sultry, sounds a bit scratchy and out of use.

"You're human?" I ask.

She bites her lip, clearly self-conscious under all our scrutiny. "Air Elemental, actually."

"How?" I manage. "How did you become a hellhound, I mean?"

And a male one at that.

"I was cursed a long time ago," she explains falteringly. She shoots glances at the others but then focuses again on me. "An evil sorceress married my father and, in her thirst to rule my kingdom after he died, doomed me to live as a hellhound bound to the library—to the confines of the ground and walls—for as long as it existed. But now…thanks to you, I'm free." Her eyes glimmer with unshed tears of gratitude.

"That's… incredible," I say.

"That's insane," Blossom adds. "She changed your species *and* your gender?" The unicorn shifter shudders. "I hope that bitch suffers."

"She will," Bingo says, eyes glittering with that promise.

Mag can only stare—until Blossom elbows him violently.

I glance at Leo, who's staring at the blonde with wide eyes, a mixture of recognition and awe dawning on his face. "Bingo?" he whispers, stepping closer.

She nods, her eyes locking onto his. "My true name is Elyra."

Some realization seems to hit Leo as his eyes widen. "That's why you followed me around all this time," he says, his voice choked with emotion. "You were my mate…even then."

Mate?

Elyra smiles, tears glistening in her eyes as she steps into his arms. "Yes," she whispers. "And now, I'm finally me again."

A quick glance reveals the others are just as shocked as I am.

Leo pulls Elyra close and kisses her, both completely lost to anything but each other.

I can't help but look over at Kitty with suspicion. "Are you cursed too?" I demand.

She meows up at me then sniffs and looks away.

"Apparently, a raccoon is just a raccoon," Blossom says.

I feel Aries's hand tighten around mine, and I turn to him, my heart swelling with love and gratitude.

"And where do you want to go, Paige Nemos?" he asks softly, his voice filled with all the promises of our future.

I smile, the answer coming to me as naturally as breathing. "Home," I say, the word warm and full of hope.

Once, I dreamt of going out in search of my place in the world. And as I stand here, surrounded by the restored Athenaeum and the people we love, I know that, no matter where we go, no matter what comes next, I've already found it.

EPILOGUE

PAIGE

Five years later

I stand at the entrance of the castle garden, watching the gnomes wrangle the kids. Three little dragons, all darting around with the boundless energy that only young ones have, weaving between trees and chasing after butterflies, or rather, attempting to torch them.

"Careful," I shout when I see a stream of fire shoot out from Aelia nearly catching a butterfly mid-flight. "Don't incinerate the wildlife!"

Ted waves his tiny arms at me as he races by on Kitty's back. "Don't worry, my lady! We've got it under control!"

Behind him, Zed is frantically trying to put out a small blaze Ignis, the oldest of the triplets, started in the bushes. Fred grabs a bucket of water, and Ned is running around with a butterfly net, trying to catch the butterflies before the children can. Or maybe he's trying to catch the children. Who knows anymore?

I press a hand to my forehead, sighing with a smile. “Under control, huh?”

Aries chuckles beside me. “We’ll owe them big for this.”

“Think they know what they’ve gotten themselves into?” I ask, watching as Ignis takes off in the air, his tiny wings flapping furiously. At four, he’s still too small for proper flight, but that doesn’t stop him from trying.

“They’ll be fine,” Aries says, grinning as he watches our brood terrorize the garden. “They’ve defended the library against all manner of threats, including a full-grown hydra. Three little dragons should be easy.”

I snort. “Sometimes, I think I’d rather face the hydra.”

Aries chuckles as Aelia lets out another burst of flame, this time singeing the gnomes’ hats as she scurries past. Queen Dorthea watches it all from her vantage point on the veranda. Solaryn is perched on her hip with a cookie in each hand and chocolate icing covering her mouth.

Queen, indeed, I think, watching Dorthea dote on her grandchildren. It’s still strange sometimes to watch the former queen of Astronia spend her days chasing her grandkids around rather than being chased by courtiers and advisors. But Dorthea seems thrilled with her retirement, even going so far as to take the triplets camping last weekend up in the foothills—a trip that resulted in her wearing pants for what was apparently the first time in her fae life.

Leo hasn’t let her live it down.

Now, watching her and the gnomes wrangle the triplets is both a joy and a bit of a disaster waiting to happen. But I shove aside the worry, grabbing Aries’ hand. “Come on, let’s go before I change my mind.”

We slip out of the garden, heading back inside where Leo and Elyra are already striding toward us hand-in-hand. The diamond on her finger gleams even from here. It’s the largest, gaudiest thing I've ever seen, but she seems to love it almost as much as she does the mate who put it there.

"Ready?" I ask.

"Yes, sorry we're late," Elyra says. She runs her hand down her green dress as if to make sure it's unruffled.

"We got held up." Leo smirks at Aries, and my mate shakes his head.

"Right on time, actually," I say, turning to the smooth section of wall and calling my magic to me. "This spot works as good as any."

With a few mental nudges to the magic, a portal appears, swirling and whirling over the wall. The surface is murky, but it's not the inky darkness that once would have given us all pause. This is a navy blue that winks with what looks a lot like stars.

A window to another world.

My home away from home.

I lead the way, stepping through with Aries' hand still firmly twined with my own. He's close behind me. Even after all this time, he won't take any chances of being separated—not by magic or anything else.

On the other side, I inhale the scent of dust and paper.

A thousand memories wash over me, as they always do when the Athenaeum first hits my senses. Blossom and Mag have made changes, but the heart of this place remains unchanged. Maybe that's why I see my childhood everywhere I look. Where it once used to feel like a prison, the library now feels like a second home. One I haven't visited nearly as often as I'd like since the triplets were born.

"It's quiet," I say as we make our way through the stacks.

"Isn't that a good thing?" Aries asks.

Behind us, Leo and Elyra step through the portal.

I glance behind them to where the magic continues to swirl, beckoning.

"You think they're going to be okay?" I ask with one last glance at the castle before it disappears behind us.

"The kids or the gnomes?" Aries teases.

"Both," I say, laughing.

"They'll survive," he assures me, smiling. "Besides, we need this break."

"Aries is right," Leo says. "Tonight, you're off duty. Now, come on, and let me pour my queen a drink."

Leo pushes past us, Elyra in tow. She tosses me an apologetic look that has me smiling ruefully. She and I have become close these past few years. That's still strange sometimes too. Knowing one of my best friends—and now sister—used to be a hellhound who was apparently just cursed and trapped into the body of one by her evil stepmother. Thanks to that nightmare, Elyra's healing is ongoing, but there's a light in her eyes that grows brighter every week.

"You up for this?" Aries asks, and I realize I've been standing still too long.

Leo and Elyra disappear around the corner, and I look over at my mate, offering him a smile. "I am."

"Because we can go home right now," he offers. "Spend the evening alone…"

"As nice as that sounds, we're here," I say pointedly. "But let's plan for that 'alone' portion when we get home."

He winks, and I tug him along toward the sound of voices.

We round the corner, and I see the others gathered around a sitting area that's been transformed since the years I called this place home. Much of the common areas have been, in fact, but the former break room is my favorite.

Twice the size of what it used to be, the space is basically a communal living area. The hard-backed chairs and scuffed tables are gone, replaced by a cozy couch and chairs scattered over a worn rug. The full-sized fridge remains though it's been updated to an industrial size with automatic dispensers and countertops lining both sides.

On the other side of the space, a long dining table with chairs enough for at least twelve has already been set and laden with food. In the far corner, a bar is stocked with drinks and snacks. Mag stands behind it, pouring and mixing cocktails.

"You made it," he calls, flashing us a handsome smile.

Aries releases my hand and makes his way to the bar, greeting Mag with some sort of special handshake.

"You're here!" Blossom grabs me in a hug, her high ponytail tickling my shoulder before she releases me.

"Why do you look so surprised?" I ask.

Blossom winces. "I actually had ten pieces on you not coming at all. I thought the little monsters would've dragged you back before you got two steps out the door."

"We considered it," I say, shaking my head. "The gnomes are probably regretting all their life choices right about now."

Mag snorts. "Those kids are nothing compared to what we've handled." His tone is gruff, but there's a twinkle in his stone eyes. "Though, from what I hear, Uncle Leo has started teaching them to fly early."

Blossom raises an eyebrow at him then me. "Already? I thought you were waiting for spring to start flight lessons."

"I was." I glare at Leo. "He had other plans."

Leo shrugs. "I'm helpless against their charms; what can I say?"

Aries returns to my side, offering me a drink. Mag follows, passing drinks to Leo and Elyra.

"The king allowed this?" Blossom asks, smirking at Aries.

He sips his drink, clearly amused. "They're eager. Can't blame them for that."

"And the fire-breathing?" Mag asks, eyes sparkling with mischief. "Have they set anything else on fire besides the garden?"

"Just the gnomes' hats," I admit.

"Ah, well, better than the whole castle, I suppose," Blossom says. "Next time you want a night out, Mag and I will babysit. At least, he can't be burnt to a crisp."

"It's a deal," I say with a laugh, but deep down, I'm so grateful that Blossom and Mag managed to synchronize the library's measurement of time to Astronia's so they can be more present for the triplets.

We all sit down at the long table, passing food and serving our own plates while we talk and laugh. The conversation flows easily, filled with lighthearted banter, shared memories, and stories of our adventures—both past and recent.

Mag shares a tale about remodeling a section of the library's lower level with only a gargoyle's brute strength, and Blossom adds her own version, full of dramatized flair and exaggerated details. Aries talks about the kids' progress in learning to fly (or lack thereof), and Leo chimes in with his grand ideas of teaching them the finer points of dragon combat. And for the first time in a long while, the weight of royal responsibilities feels far away.

Aries squeezes my hand again, and when I look at him, his smile is soft, content, like he's thinking the same thing I am: This is what we've been fighting for.

I glance around at our little group—Aries, Leo, Elyra, Blossom, and Mag, not just friends but family—all of us safe, happy, together. And I think: This is what the stories meant about a happily ever after. Against all odds, and with a little help from some pumpkin spice and accidental alchemy, I found my happy ending. Except it's not an ending at all, it's just the beginning.

Want more romantasy from Heather Hildenbrand?
Snag the free prequel A GLAMOUR OF SMOKE & SHADOW
and dive into the world of the Cursed Fae where enemies

become lovers and bullies become the greatest villain the realm has ever known.

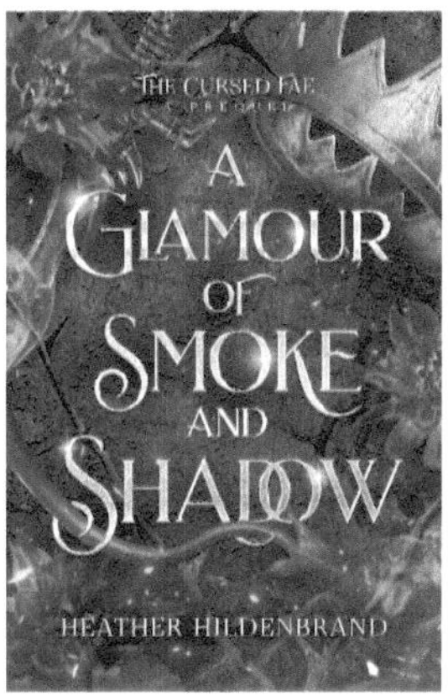

THE AINE ARE AN ELITE CASTE OF WARRIORS AMONG THE FAE. A sacred dozen selected by the Fates to protect this world.

Today, I join my sisters and become one of them.

It's all I've ever wanted.

Then *he* shows up.

The Furiosities are demon-gods. The three kings of Hel, they call them. No mortal fae has ever laid eyes on them before today, though their cruelty and wrath are legendary.

The first two make me want to run in the other direction, but the moment I lay eyes on the third male, everything else falls away.

Dark, mesmerizing, and intense—he is more than forbidden to someone like me. He is impossible.

Yet, when he speaks, I know I will do anything he asks. Even break my most sacred vow.

My weapons and magic might belong to my people, but my body and heart are owned by another—and there's no telling how the demon-god might bend or break both in the end.

. . .

Turn the page for a sneak peek….

A GLAMOUR OF SMOKE & SHADOW

The eyes of the Fates are fixed on me.

I don't look over at them to acknowledge their presence though every ounce of protocol requires me to do so. To ignore the Fates is to insult the goddesses of creation. But today's an exception to formality. Besides, I've trained my whole life for this chance. I refuse to let manners ruin it for me. So, I concentrate instead on winning this fight.

Late afternoon sun trickles in between the leafy branches overhead. The warm, humid air of summer has already made my skin sticky, though some of that is probably nerves. Beneath my feet, the ground has been cleared down to nothing but dirt. The space here is dubbed the warrior's circle. Surrounding it, fae and forest alike press in at the edges.

Everyone has come to watch us, but I shut them out easily enough. The Fates' presence is the only distraction for me.

Crouched in the center of the circle, my opponent, Heliconia, shows none of the conflict I feel at ignoring the three deities watching from the sidelines. Instead, she glares at me with the fires of Hel burning in her dark gaze. If I hadn't lived and sparred with Heliconia for the last six months, I'd worry she had Furiosity blood running through those fae veins.

Her temper never wanes. Her strength is unmatched. She's a fae warrior from the strongest bloodlines, a formidable foe, but I'm determined to beat her today.

My future is riding on my victory. All I've ever wanted is to become one of the Aine. Now, the only thing standing in my way is Heliconia Kucera.

"A moment please." The three Fates—willowy figures that depict the maiden, mother, and crone—speak as one. Their combined voice is an ethereal blend of the three goddesses.

I've only seen them once in my life before this moment.

The day they selected me to compete is still imprinted in my mind like a fever dream. My family comes from warriors, sure, but this is an honor few have received. My parents cried for days afterward, and my village threw me a parade before I left for training just outside our realm's capital city. At the time, all the attention embarrassed me, but the memory of my people's pride has carried me through the most brutal training I've ever endured.

Six months later, the Fates have come to Sevanwinds, the summer kingdom, to preside over our final competition. Those who make it will be divided into four groups. Three of us will remain in Sevanwinds to serve the crown here. The other three groups will be sent to the remaining kingdoms—fall, winter, spring—and pledge themselves to a king or queen there. The Aine have kept peace among the kingdoms for centuries this way. My generation will be no different.

My two best friends, Lesha and Amanti, have already won their rounds and secured their place as an Aine. There's only one spot left, and it's down to me and Heliconia. Twelve Aine—timeless, immortal warriors. Female fae of the highest honor. When our transformation is finished, we'll be full-blooded Fairies. Chosen by the Fates themselves to protect this world.

I want that twelfth spot more than I've ever wanted anything.

Right now, the Fates' sudden interruption grates against my already taut nerves, but I respectfully turn to them as they continue their announcement. "Before we begin the last round, the Furiosities wish to join us and observe this sacred rite of selection."

Their voices are pleasant, but shock and dread shoot through me.

Heliconia and I exchange a look.

"Are they serious?" she whispers, eyes wide.

"I don't think they'd lie," I say, just as surprised.

Murmurs erupt from the crowd that's gathered to witness this last battle. The Fates don't bother to shush them. A moment later, behind the circle of onlookers, smoke rises, thick and dark, from the earth.

Heliconia and I step back, shoulder to shoulder, allies now should we need to be. She's a warrior fae like me. A sister. Or she might've been if we hadn't been brought to this moment—forced to become opponents.

Inside the black smoke, a trio of figures appear. They stand close until their forms solidify. Then, out of the smoke, three males emerge. I have no idea what the protocol is for looking directly at a Furiosity. They are demon-gods. The kings of Hel. No living fae has seen them, though tales of their wrath and cruelty are legendary. In villages, stories of the Furiosities keep children from misbehaving. I'd always thought them closer to fantasy than reality. Yet, here they are.

According to legend, they've never attended an Aine selection.

Until now.

They turn to face the Fates, offering a short bow and exchanging words in a language I don't recognize. The Furiosities' voices are low and deep, sending shudders through me that conjure images of black flames and eternal torture. And power. Pure, limitless power.

Then, they stride over to Heliconia and me.

The crowd parts for them in utter silence.

My breath catches, sticking in my lungs under the weight of their dark stares.

"You are the remaining contenders?" one of them demands roughly. He's an old man, though his shoulders are broad and his posture strong.

"Yes," Heliconia says, saving me from a response.

"I am Age," he says, a nasty glint in his murky eyes.

The male beside him is middle-aged with brown skin and a cruel snarl. "I am Eld." He glances from Heliconia to me, and it takes all my courage not to shrink away.

The third male is younger than the others. In fact, he appears to be in his mid-twenties like me. He studies me with an intensity that makes my palms sweat. His hair is dark and messy, falling carelessly over his ears. He is handsome, though it's more than that—a magnetism that has me staring far longer than I should.

"I am Ire." His voice is low, his full mouth mesmerizing as it moves.

A nasty scar runs down his jawline near his ear. Before I realize what I'm doing, I lift my hand and press a finger to the jagged mark.

The crowd gasps.

I yank my hand back, coming to my senses with utter and total horror. "My apologies, I… I have no idea why I did that."

Beside me, Heliconia shifts her weight, and I know she's celebrating her victory. I can't blame her. I'm already dead. She won't even have to fight me. The demon-god will destroy me for her.

"What is your name, little warrior?" the one called Ire asks.

"Sonoma Eko," I whisper, still bracing for certain death.

They say Furiosities can kill with a single blow. Hopefully, that means it'll be painless.

"Sonoma," he repeats, the sound of my name in his voice sending trembles through me that have nothing to do with fear. I lower my face, hiding the flush spreading over my cheeks. "You shouldn't bother being envious of my scars. From the looks of that one, you'll have your own soon enough."

My eyes jerk back to his.

Beside me, Heliconia grins smugly.

He chuckles. They all do. Then, they step back, retreating to the edge of the circle where the Fates wait.

I watch in disbelief, still not quite ready to accept he isn't going to kill me where I stand.

"Are both warriors ready?" the Fates ask.

Heliconia backs away from me so she can take up her previous stance. Her eyes glint with determination. "Ready," she calls.

I'm still regaining my focus when the Fates say, "Begin!"

Heliconia is a tornado, arms and legs moving faster than I can block. She sees my hesitation and exploits it mercilessly.

From the sidelines, the crowd screams, cheering for their favorite. Their voices become a roar as Heliconia's fist slams into my jaw, and I'm driven backward.

My feet stumble. Panic rises in me. My distraction has cost me. And we've only just begun.

ABOUT THE AUTHOR

Heather Hildenbrand lives in coastal Virginia where she writes paranormal and fantasy romance full of enemies to lovers and heroes who brood. Her most frequent hobbies are cuddling with her 100-pound goldendoodle, riding country roads on the back of her husband's motorcycle, and avoiding killer slugs.

You can find out more about Heather and her books at www.heatherhildenbrand.com.

ALSO BY HEATHER HILDENBRAND

Dark Wolf Soul

Deadly Wolf Bite

Broken Wolf Heart

Kingdom of Briars and Roses (Cursed Fae)

A Glamour of Smoke and Shadow (Cursed Fae)

Protect Me (Immortal Vices & Virtues)

Hunt Me (Immortal Vices & Virtues)

Consume Me (Immortal Vices & Virtues) - coming 2025

To Hunt A Wolf

To Kiss A Wolf

To Keep A Wolf

Midnight Cursed

Midnight Hunted

Midnight Bound

Wolf Cursed

Wolf Captive

Wolf Chosen

Wolf Revealed

A Witch's Call

A Witch's Destiny

A Witch's Fate

A Witch's Soul

A Witch's Prophecy

A Witch's Hope

Twisted Tides

The Girl Who Cried Werewolf

The Girl Who Cried Captive

The Girl Who Cried War

The Girl Who Never Cried

The Winter Witch

The Spring Witch

The Witch's Heart

Midnight Mate

One Dark Spark

Two Blazing Hearts

Three Scorched Kingdoms

Goddess Ascending

Goddess Claiming

Goddess Forging

Kiss of Death

Knock Em Dead

Death's Door

Dead to Rights

Dead End

The Girl Who Called The Stars

The Girl Who Ruled The Stars

Alpha Games

Alpha Trials

Alpha Chosen

Dirty Blood

Cold Blood

Blood Bond

Blood Rule

Broken Blood

Imitation

Deviation

Generation

Heather also writes small town contemporary romance as Violet Stafford.

Stay For Summer

The Breakup Bet

www.ingramcontent.com/pod-product-compliance
Lightning Source LLC
Chambersburg PA
CBHW020335310726
48979CB00015B/2383/J
* 9 7 8 1 9 6 1 4 5 5 3 1 3 *